TIME FOR US
Copyright © 2018 C. Kaye
All rights reserved.
Published by C. Kaye Books

ISBN: 978-0-9982167-4-4
Print ISBN: 978-0-9982167-5-1

This is a work of fiction. Names, characters, places and incidents are either the product of the author's imagination or are used fictitiously, and any resemblance to actual persons, living or dead, business establishments, events or locales is entirely coincidental.

Printed in the USA.
Developmental Editing by A Book A Day Author Services

Cover Design and Interior Format
© THE KILLION GROUP INC.

Time FOR US

OUR TIME FOR LOVE #2

C. KAYE

To my dear friend Odessa Jones.
You were the inspiration for Tiba.
I will forever miss your spunk and charm.
RIP my dear friend, you
will always be loved!

"It's one of the greatest gifts you can give yourself, to forgive. Forgive everybody."
—Maya Angelou

Prologue

MAX

TWINKLE LIGHTS, PINK FLOWERS, DANCING, laughter … It was more than I could take. So, here I am in the barn shoveling horse manure and trying to be happy for Gemma. She seems to love Raef and after all, he is Charley's father. It's hard, having loved Gemma for as long as I can remember. Mom says I just *think* I'm in love and I've become used to being there for Gemma and Charley. Mom's crazy because I know how I feel and I know I love Gemma.

I hear something from the other end of the barn, so I step out of the stall. Tiba heads my way, looking down and tip-toeing the entire time. For some reason, the sight makes me chuckle. She looks up when she hears me.

"What's so funny, big guy?" Tiba asks with a smile. I decide to make it easier and go to her so she doesn't have to come any farther into the barn.

"Just the sight of you in your dress and heels walking in the barn."

"Well, the last thing I want is horse shit on my good shoes!" she responds indignantly but with a smirk.

"Can't have horse shit on a princess now can we?"

"I am so far from a princess and you know it. But I do love shoes and these are some fine shoes!" Tiba points to her feet. I look down and see she is right. They are some very sexy shoes. The kind of shoes I would want a woman to wear when she has nothing else on. There is a sudden flash in my mind of Tiba doing just that. Where did that thought come from?

"So, enough about shoes. What tore you away from Moss and brought you out here?" Moss has been hanging all over Tiba since last night at the bar. The dude has gotten on my nerves with that. He will leave tomorrow and Tiba will still be here. Why can't he just leave her alone? It's none of my business, but his blatant pursuit of her is driving me crazy today. You would think I'm jealous of him, but that's a crazy thought. Why would I be jealous? Or am I?

"No one had to *tear me away* from Moss, silly man. I'm out here because Charley is looking for you. She wants to dance with you." Tiba reaches down to pull hay out of her shoe. My mind flashes again to her with nothing on but those shoes. What is wrong with me? This wedding must have my brain completely crazy!

"I've had enough happiness for one day. Plus, I've been shoveling horse shit as you put it. I probably smell pretty bad by now." I don't want to disappoint Charley, but I don't want to go back to the reception either.

Suddenly, I feel hands on my arms. Tiba leans her head to my chest and her nose rubs my shirt as she smells me. She smells me! What the hell? Tiba grips my arms tighter and takes one last breath before she backs away. Before I realize it, I have my hands on her waist and pull her a step closer to me. My heart beats faster in my chest and my head is fuzzy. *Am I about to pass out?* What a crazy thought!

"You smell pretty good to me, big guy." Tiba smirks as she looks up with her big chocolate eyes. I never noticed the flecks of gold amid the brown. The combination is striking and I can't seem to tear my eyes away from hers. I also can't seem to find my voice. I merely stare back at her while she continues. "So, why don't you go make your niece a very happy little girl and dance with her."

"You have beautiful eyes," I hear myself say but it doesn't sound like my voice. What is wrong with me? I can't breathe. My heart is about to jump out of my chest. Maybe I'm having a heart attack. That's it. I should ask Tiba to go get help. I can't get myself to say that, though. Instead, her lips catch my attention and all I want to do is kiss her. Tiba has managed to take my mind off my earlier stress and put my thoughts squarely on her, even though I don't know why or how. The urge to feel her lips rushes through me and I hear myself say, "I really want to kiss you right now."

Tiba's eyes never leave mine and the gold flecks seem to dance. Her face gets closer as she stands on her toes and leans into me.

"Then why don't you?"

Before I can stop myself, I pull Tiba flush to my body and dip my head to hers. When our lips connect, my entire body burns like it is a smoldering fire. My heart beats even faster. I can't seem to control myself and the kiss quickly spirals with passion. My tongue slips in and finds hers. She meets me every step of the way. What I feel in this moment is something I've never felt with a kiss. Tiba's body fits mine perfectly and I press her even tighter into me. Her palms roam my chest, leaving sparks in their wake. My hands are in the spirals of her curly hair, holding her mouth to mine.

Tiba pulls back and I let her. I need to breathe. We gaze into each other's eyes as we catch our breath. Her eyes are glazed and her lips swollen. She seems to be as affected by this as I am. As if sensing my thoughts, Tiba takes a step back from me. Fighting the urge to pull her back to me, I watch as she smooths her dress with her hands and then attempts to straighten her hair. I notice a smear of her lipstick and reach out to wipe it away. She lets me, but then takes another step back.

"Um, you need to come out and see Charley." Tiba turns away from me and heads quickly to the door of the barn.

"Tiba, wait!" I call after her, but she doesn't stop as she runs out the barn door.

In that moment, I decide that I *will* go out and see Charley. I don't want to disappoint her and for some reason, I don't want to disappoint Tiba. Looking down, I realize I need a few more minutes before I go anywhere. That kiss left me hard and anxious. My mind goes back to Tiba's body pressed against mine and I feel myself harden even more. Dammit, I can't think of that and go anywhere!

I attempt to convince myself to think of something other than Tiba, but I can't seem to tear my mind away from her.

What the hell just happened here?

Chapter 1

MAX

Three months later

TAPPING MY BEER BOTTLE ON the counter, I catch the attention of the bartender. He nods and quickly replaces the empty bottle with a new one. No words are needed between us. I have become a frequent visitor over the last few months and have befriended the entire bar staff. My life has become work during the day and attempting to drink away my thoughts at night. That's probably not the best way to live but I haven't cared much about anything lately.

It has been three months since Gemma married Raef. Three months since my ex-wife, the only woman I've ever loved, married her prince charming.

Gemma's parents died when she was 18 and as an only child with no other family, one horrific moment left her all alone. Our families had always been close, so Gemma and I had always been best friends. I'll freely admit that I took a tragic event and used it as an opportunity to convince her to marry me. Even though I tried to make it work and hoped Gemma would learn to love me, she never felt *that* way. I never told her how I felt about her back then, never saying the words, "I love you." Instead, I waited until the week she was about to marry another man to drop that little bomb on her. Not the smartest move I've ever made. To Gemma I'm nothing more than I've ever been: a best friend. Hell, she says she considers me like a brother.

Gemma and Raef belong together, I see that now. He's the father of her daughter, Charley, and it's obvious they love each other. They've been very kind to not kick me completely out of their lives after my stunt. They accepted my apology for trying to come between them and still accept me as their friend. Gemma even continues to allow me to be 'Uncle Max' to Charley, for which I'm very grateful because I can't imagine my life without that little munchkin in it. I've adjusted to Raef being a part of their lives and even find myself liking the dude.

This whole situation is the reason I find myself at the bar each evening. I seem to have spent the last five or so years doing the best I can at screwing up my life. Now, I can't seem to figure out how to move forward. My professional life may be going well, but my personal life is a wreck.

I tilt the beer bottle back for another drink. Out of the corner of my eye, I notice a couple move in beside me at the bar. Not being in a particularly social mood, I ignore them. That is until I hear my name.

"Max?" the person next to me questions.

I take one more swig from my beer before turning to the man. I'm shocked when I see Raef's friend Moss.

"Moss," I respond as I shake his hand. "What the hell are you doing in Granier? Thought you went back to Chicago."

"I'm just here for a few days. I've decided to try to spend a little more time in New Orleans than I have the last few years. I ran over here to visit Raef, Gemma, and Charley." Moss turns to the woman by his side. "Plus, it gave me an excuse to take this beauty out for dinner and drinks."

My eyes move to the woman with Moss and my chest tightens when I realize the woman is Tiba. The woman who is another reason I have spent every night in this bar. The woman I kissed the day of Gemma's wedding who ran away from me afterward. The woman I haven't been able to get out of my mind even though I've avoided her since that day. I can't avoid her now, but instead drink in the sight of her. She is just as beautiful as she was that day.

"Hey, Tiba. How've you been?" I ask, hoping she didn't see the shock on my face before I could hide it.

"I've been great. How about you?" Tiba smiles and my heart races. She turns to Moss and smiles even bigger at him. I feel like someone punched me in the gut. I don't like the way she looks at him. Even worse, I don't like how it makes me feel. I have spent the last few months trying to under-stand why I keep thinking about kissing Tiba when I love Gemma. Is it because Gemma is now Raef's and I know I can't have her? Or could my crazy mother be right and I don't love Gemma quite the way I thought I did?

"So, been waiting on Moss to come back since the wedding, huh?" My tone is sarcastic as I grab my beer.

Tiba looks back to me with her lips in a tight line and one eyebrow raised. She doesn't respond. Moss chuckles and drops his arm behind Tiba on her bar stool. I grip my beer bottle even tighter. Why does this guy keep showing up and giving Tiba all this attention? He's just going to leave again. *Why do I care? Why am I worried about who Tiba sees?* My mind attempts to remind me that I'm not supposed to think about Tiba. Something it has been doing on a regular basis lately.

"I don't think she's been waiting on me at all," Moss says as he chuckles again. I sure wish I knew what this man finds so damn funny.

Tiba still says nothing but turns her attention to the bar. Moss motions to the bartender and orders their drinks, giving me the opportunity to turn away from them and cut off the conversation. I didn't come here to visit. I finish off my beer and motion for another. With all the stress I've felt the last couple of months, Tiba has crept into my thoughts all too frequently. Convincing myself that the amazing kiss we shared was just a fluke, I've not let myself think about what might have happened had she not run out of the barn that day. Instead, I've kept myself away from her.

Moss and Tiba chat while I brood. Moss is a nice guy and I like him. I just don't like him with Tiba. My thoughts drift back to the barn at my parents' house. I think of how beautiful Tiba looked in that pink dress with those heels. *Those shoes.* That thought has my eyes drift down to see what she has on her feet tonight and I see another pair of heels. These are red and sky high. *Damn, what I could do to her in those shoes.*

With a shake of my head, I wonder why I have these thoughts about Tiba. Before that day at the wedding, I'd never looked at her that way. After the kiss, I've tried to convince myself it was a one-time thing from the emotions of the day, but here I am, yet again, imagining her with nothing on but her shoes. I really think I'm losing my mind.

Finishing off my beer, I throw money for my night on the bar. I need to get away from Moss and Tiba. I also need to call someone to pick me up. Too much beer was consumed tonight for me to drive home. That's another thing that has become regular in my life lately, and I think the guys at work have had enough of it. They seem edgy when they have to pick me up. This mess—the way I handled Gemma's marriage and the subsequent kiss with Tiba—has had me in a downward spiral. I need to pull my life together soon or I won't have any workers left on my jobs.

Before I can get away from the bar, Moss stops me. "Leaving, man? You're not driving, are you?"

"Nah. I'll call someone to pick me up."

"Ride with us. We're about to leave."

My head jerks toward Tiba at Moss's words. The last thing I want to do is get in a vehicle with these two.

"Thanks for the offer but I live outside of town. Don't want to put you out." My focus is still on Tiba and she gives me a smirk.

"Ride with us, big guy," Tiba says before she pulls her eyes away from mine. To Moss she continues.

"You can drop us both at my place and I'll take Max on to his house. That way you won't be so late getting back to the city."

My heart jolts at the thought of being alone again with Tiba. The only thing I can think of right now is having the opportunity to kiss her again. Why do these thoughts keep popping up in my mind? At least this time, I didn't blurt it out. Once again, I wonder if I've boarded the crazy train. Maybe it's just the alcohol this time. Before I can pull out of my thoughts and say something to stop this nonsense, Moss responds.

"Sounds like a plan." Moss tosses a few bills on the bar. He places his hand on the small of Tiba's back as they move toward the door. Rooted in place, my eyes are glued to where his hand touches her. When I don't follow, he looks over his shoulder. "Come on, Max. You're riding with us."

As my eyes raise from Tiba's back, I see she is also looking over her shoulder and sees me watching her. She takes a small step away from Moss and his hand drops to his side. That encourages me to move. Tiba waits for me to catch up and when I am next to her, she gives me a smile that lights up her entire face. She leans closer to me and whispers, "Don't worry, I won't bite."

My mouth falls open in shock while Tiba throws back her head and laughs. The sound is musical and I find myself suddenly wanting to hear it again.

Moss is oblivious to what was said since he is already at the door. He holds it open for us to pass through. If I didn't know better, I would think his date was flirting with me, yet he seems unfazed by Tiba's actions.

When we reach Moss's vehicle, Tiba insists on being in the back to let me ride up front. While I find it odd, I don't argue. This entire night has me out of sorts to the point I don't know what is up or what is down. Moss helps Tiba in before climbing into the driver's seat. I settle in the passenger seat and take in the interior of the vehicle. It has nice leather seats and seems to have all kinds of bells and whistles. Moss notices my observations and laughs.

"I know this isn't what you're used to. I'm just not a truck guy. A small SUV is about as big as I want to drive." Moss motions with his hand around the interior. He is a city guy and the Audi fits him perfectly, but it definitely isn't my taste. It makes me feel even more out of my element tonight.

"It's nice," I respond.

Moss makes small talk on the drive to Tiba's apartment. Fortunately, she doesn't live far, so I don't have to suffer through much conversation. The mood in the vehicle is awkward for me, but Moss and Tiba seem completely comfortable. I breathe a sigh of relief when we pull into the parking lot and I jump out of the vehicle as soon as it comes to a stop.

Moss opens the door for Tiba and helps her out. They talk so softly I can't hear what they say. After a few moments, he gives her a quick hug that doesn't seem intimate at all. I'm relieved that I didn't have to witness them kiss. Tiba walks around the car toward me as she waves to Moss.

"See you later, Max," Moss says as he opens his car door.

"Thanks for the ride."

Tiba is now beside me and we both watch Moss

pull out of the parking lot. She turns to face me after he is out of sight.

"Well, big guy. Looks like it's just you and me."

Chapter 2

TIBA

WHY DO I FEEL LIKE I just threw down the gauntlet? It was a spur of the moment decision to bring Max here under the guise of taking him home. My real intention was not to take him anywhere, but to convince him to stay. Now he stands before me with his brow furrowed in an expression of shock and something else I can't decipher. It almost looks like fear. Fear is something I've never seen on Max Greenwood.

Max continues to stare at me without speaking. Maybe I've read him wrong and the kiss we shared didn't mean anything to him. Boy, what a kiss it was though. I've thought about little else since that day. Now is not the time to back down from what I want regardless of Max's silence.

"So, you want to come inside?" I ask as I tilt my head to the side. Max's eyes widen and his mouth opens as if he's about to say something but stops. Confusion shows in his frown and he appears to wage an internal battle on how to respond. My gaze stays locked with his until he finally tears his eyes away from mine.

"Umm, okay." It's not exactly the reaction I

hoped for, but it isn't a no either.

I motion toward the apartment and we walk that direction. I stay quiet to allow Max time to decide if this is really what he wants to do. As we climb the stairs to my second-floor home, Max breaks the silence.

"Was that a date?"

"What? Moss?" Max nods, but I shake my head. "Definitely not a date. Moss and I became fast friends with the wedding festivities but that's all we are and all we'll ever be."

"Oh. I thought he was interested in you."

"He may have been at first, but we got that straightened out at the wedding." I laugh when I think about that conversation with Moss. I can't tell Max that it centered around him. Moss noticed my eyes typically followed Max and bluntly asked me about my interest in him. The last thing I wanted to do was admit just how crazy I am about the big guy, but I did. Even though I'd never shared my feelings for Max with anyone, I wound up spilling everything. Moss listened and assured me my secret was safe with him. Shortly after that chat, I made my fateful trek to the barn.

We arrive at my door and I shuffle everything in my purse to find my key. Max stands patiently, watching with interest. When I can't find the stupid thing, Max seems to find it humorous.

"What all do you have in there?" He leans over to look inside my purse.

"Everything I might need! A woman has to be prepared." Just at that moment, my hand locates my keychain. "*Voila!* Keys!"

Making quick work of the lock we enter my little apartment. I turn on the lamp next to the door and Max looks around the small living room. I try to view my home as he sees it. It's tiny, but I can't afford much. I may have a messy purse, but I keep my little place immaculate. I begin to feel a bit self-conscious as Max continues to look around without speaking.

"It's not much but it's safe. That's what I was looking for when I got this place." I motion around the apartment. Only Gemma knows why I need a safe place and I plan to keep it that way. My past is just that, but because of it, safety is one of my top priorities.

"It's nice." Max steps across the room to look at the pictures on my wall. "These are awesome photos. Where'd you find them?" He gives me a glance before he turns back to the wall. My gaze follows his to the black and white framed pictures of sites around New Orleans and Granier.

"I took them. I dabble in photography for fun." I look fondly at the photos, remembering the moment I took each one of them.

"You took these?" Respect shines in Max's expression and it pleases me. "Wow! They are amazing. You should do this professionally."
"I'm a long way from that. I do it for fun. I'm afraid if I ever did it for money, it wouldn't be fun anymore." What I don't tell him is the fear I have of anyone finding where I live. Time to change the subject.

Max steps closer to me before I can come up with anything else to say. When he is inches from me he places his hands on my arms, gently caressing them. I don't breathe for fear he will stop. My eyes raise to meet his and desire shines in them. I move closer to him and place my hands on his chest. Goodness what a chest this man has. His heart beats faster under my fingers.

"I don't know what you do to me, but you make me crazy," Max says as he pulls me against him. "I can't stop thinking about you."

"Seems I have the same problem." I run my hands across his chest and then up to his shoulders. His hands are on my back, teasing lightly in circles.

"Can I kiss you again?" Max asks. He leans his face toward mine. Instead of answering with words, I take my hands and place them on either side of his face to pull him to me and slowly touch my lips to his.

Max's hands still as he pulls me tighter against his body. The kiss is soft and gentle but it's enough to feel like I have electrical currents flowing through my body.

"I like the way you say yes," Max says against my lips with a grin.

We continue soft, gentle kisses. The experience is so different from the kiss in the barn, but it is no less passionate. Max has my body flush with his and I can feel every inch of his thickness against me.

"I want you, Tiba," Max tells me as he pulls his lips away from mine. "I've wanted you since we kissed in the barn."

"I want you too, Max." If he only knew just how much I do want him.

"I can't promise you more than tonight. I'm not in a good place right now." Max kisses me harder.

"I know," I say quietly against his lips, knowing how he feels about Gemma. I've secretly wanted him for so long that one night will just have to suffice. It's better than not having him at all.

Max groans against my lips when he hears my response. His tongue skims my lips and I open for him. Our tongues tangle as he eases me down to the couch. He pulls away long enough to remove my shirt. He gasps when he realizes I'm not wearing a bra.

"Damn, you're beautiful!"

"Thanks, big guy. You aren't bad yourself."

I unbutton Max's shirt to get my hands inside. Did I mention this man has one awesome chest? Max inches me back on the couch until he hovers over me. Suddenly we are kissing with more passion than before. His calloused hands roam my skin, stopping only long enough to allow me to push his shirt down his arms. My fingers glide over every muscle in his upper body. Max shifts us to where is he now completely on top of me. I'm so much smaller than he is, but it feels like we fit perfectly.

Kisses trail down my neck to my breasts. Max spends a short time there with his hands and lips before he trails further down my stomach. The roughness of his hands causes chills as he drags them along my skin. Oh, how long I've waited to feel those hands. Max raises his body to remove my skirt. It's a long one today and is now bunched up at my thighs. As he eases it down my legs, his eyes lift to mine.

"Keep the shoes on. I've had thoughts of you in nothing but heels for weeks." Max gives me a wicked smile to go along with his words. Before I know it, I am lying before him in nothing but my shoes. I should feel self-conscious, but with the way Max looks at me I don't feel anything but sexy.

My hands run down Max's sides and his eyes close as his breath catches. His fingertips tease the inside of my legs as light as feathers. Back and forth they move, edging closer to where I want them to land. I squirm below Max while he continues to tease me. A groan of pleasure escapes me when he finally moves his lips back to my breasts. One hand slides under me and lifts my body tightly against him. The other hand continues to caress my leg.

"I want to taste you," Max says as his kisses move lower along my body. His words and the thought of him *there* makes me tingle all over. My desire is off the charts. Squirming against him again, I let him know I am all for that. His mouth finally arrives where he wants it, where I want it even more. One swipe of his tongue against me and I all but fly off the couch. I can feel his smile against me before he dives back in. My hands grip the couch as Max devours me. It takes only minutes before I succumb to the pleasure and explode against him.

Max stands and quickly removes his pants, grabbing a condom from his wallet at the same time. He sheaths himself and kneels on the couch between my legs. One look confirms what I felt earlier. This man is huge. He leans over me and kisses me, hard.

"You taste like heaven," Max mumbles against my lips. "I can't wait to feel you. Tell me you want this as much as I do."

"Yes. Yes, Max. I want you." My fingers run through his hair and I kiss him back with all the passion I feel.

I moan when I feel Max at my entrance. He's so

large I worry I won't be able to handle him, especially since it has been quite some time since I've been with anyone. He begins to work his way in me, slowly. It is painful, but the pain feels so good. That fine line between pain and pleasure is so far over the pleasure side right now. After a few minutes, he is finally all the way in. He stills once he is fully seated inside my body. The fullness is amazing.

"Damn, Tiba. You feel even better than I imagined." Max begins to move inside me slowly. I wrap my legs around him and he groans as the heels he made me leave on rub against his back. His movements quickly become frenzied and soon, I topple over the edge again. My orgasm seems to go on forever, like none I've ever experienced. Max says my name loudly as he gives in to his own pleasure. The feeling of him as he lets go inside me is enough to spur another orgasm from me. The pleasure is almost too much. For a moment, I wonder if I will lose consciousness. As we come down from the intenseness of the moment, Max rolls us on our sides.

"That was amazing," Max whispers in my ear.

"Amazing," I repeat breathlessly. My mind can't form any other words. My legs are still wrapped around Max and he is still inside me. My head rests on his arm and my cheek on his chest. His fingers leisurely trail up and down my back. We stay like this for a few minutes before he slowly extricates himself from my body. I feel the loss immediately.

"I need to get rid of this." Max removes the condom and looks at me with a question in his eyes. Still unable to get words out of my mouth, I point to the door of the bathroom.

While he's gone, I have a moment to process what just happened. I just had the best sex of my life and it was with Max Greenwood. I have wanted that man for so long, but never did I imagine it would actually happen. I quickly remind myself that this was a one-time deal. Max made that clear. I am so deep in my thoughts I don't realize Max is back in the room until he takes my foot in his hands and removes my shoe. He does the same with the other foot, all the while giving me that wicked grin of his. He raises an eyebrow as he holds the shoe up before it drops back to the floor. He slides back beside me on the couch.

"Where'd you go? You seemed a thousand miles away," Max asks as he pulls me back against him.

"Hmmm." I hum against his chest. "Just still floating, I guess."

"That was definitely something. I am totally relaxed right now." Max kisses the top of my head.

My fingers venture lightly along the side of his chest, next to my face. His heartbeat slows as we lay in silence. Soon his breaths even out and he begins to quietly snore. I smile against his chest and still my fingers. It may have been just one night, but Max has fallen asleep with me in his arms. I memorize how his body feels wrapped around mine so I can remember this moment. I drift off to sleep, my smile still affixed to my face.

Chapter 3

MAX

I WAKE WITH A START. CONFUSED for a moment, I view my surroundings. Realization hits me when I feel a warm body wrapped in mine. My eyes drop and find Tiba peacefully asleep on my arm with her arm lightly resting on my side.

As much as I know I should remove myself from her, I can't help but gaze for a moment at the beautiful women in my arms. Her skin is the color of caramel, so evenly colored you can't find a blemish anywhere. Her wild hair is splayed across my arm and the pillow beneath it. A piece of hair has fallen in her face and I gently move it, stroking the side of her face in the process. She moans in her sleep and shifts her body against me.

As much as I don't want to, I ease myself from Tiba's body and off the couch. She doesn't stir. I grab a blanket off the back of the couch and cover her sexy body. She snuggles into the back of the couch, still asleep. My clothes are in a pile on the floor so it's easy for me to quickly dress. Leaning over, I lightly kiss Tiba's cheek. If it wasn't for work today, I would wake her up with a kiss and spend the morning worshiping that alluring body of hers.

"Best night ever," I whisper in her ear. It's true. Last night was the best night of my life. Who would have ever guessed? I almost regret telling her it would be a one-time thing. I shake my head to dispel that thought and remind myself that I'm nowhere close to being ready for a relationship with anyone, especially Tiba.

Grabbing my phone from the coffee table, I let myself out of the apartment. I pause at the door and take one last look at the beauty asleep on the couch. Once the door is locked behind me, I realize I have no way to leave since I rode here last night with Tiba and Moss.

A glance to my watch tells me it's only five in the morning. All the guys from work will be at the job site at six, so the last thing any of them are going to want to do is pick me up right now. I quickly decide I'll suck it up and walk back to the bar. It's only a couple of miles so I head off in that direction.

Fortunately, the town is still quiet this time of morning and I don't see anyone I know during the walk. By the time I make it to my truck, there's no time to go home and shower, so I head straight to the job site on the other side of town.

My thoughts on the drive are all about Tiba, how she tasted, how she felt around me, the sounds she made when she came. Those thoughts make me shift in my seat to find comfort as I harden in my jeans. *What the hell have I done? This was Tiba, not some random woman.* That thought is like a slap in the face.

Pulling into the job site, I wonder how I am going to handle being around Tiba in the social settings we will surely face. Hell, my mother regularly invites her to Sunday dinner. I have skipped them to avoid her after the wedding, so I guess I'll just keep doing that. That will work until Mom has enough of it and forces me to show up. Once again, I seem to have screwed my life, literally this time. But damn it was good.

I slam my hand against the steering wheel in frustration when I park. There has to be a way to put those thoughts out of my mind. I warned Tiba that it would only be last night. She was aware, and she still went along with it. We can be adults and face each other after a one-night stand. Hell, I've had many of those. But has Tiba?

Why does my conscious have to show up now? Adults. We are adults and this will all be fine. I grab my hard hat and slam the truck door behind me.

"What'd that truck eva' do to ya'?" Jerry's words cause me to jump. I look over my shoulder and see him point to the truck door. "Bad night?"

"Something like that." I don't look him in the eyes. Jerry has been with Greenwood Construction since I was a kid and would come to the job sites with my dad. I may be his boss now, but he's still a father figure to me. He doesn't let me forget it either and I don't like to disappoint him any more than I do my own father.

"Same clothes ya' were in yesterday too."

I don't respond. There's no point. He knows it's true. We fall in step beside each other. Before we walk in the gate of the construction zone, Jerry grabs my shoulder and stops me. This means he has something to say that I probably don't want to hear.

"Son, ya' know I respect ya', right?" I nod. "And ya' know I think of ya' like one of ma' own boys?" I nod again. "Well, I'm gonna' tell ya' what I'd tell one of them. Get ya' shit together. You're drinkin' too much, mopin' too much. It's your life, but when it starts affectin' ya' here at work, it's time to stop."

Dropping my head in shame, I nod. Jerry is right. I do need to get my shit together. "Yes, sir. You're right. I'll do better."

"Your dad built this company from the ground up. I just don't want to see ya' mess that up." Jerry pats my shoulder before he heads in the gate.

Hanging back a few minutes, I think about his words. My life has spun out control lately, but I didn't realize it had impacted things here at work. This was always the one place that was going right for me. To hear Jerry tell me that even this is spiraling was hard to hear. I *can't* let my personal life spill over to the company. Jerry is absolutely correct about that. If I am going to change my life, I have to start right here. This company is my legacy from my father and I will not disappoint him.

Today begins a new day. I head in the gate to start putting my life back together, one piece at a time.

Chapter 4

TIBA

LIGHT FROM THE WINDOW FILLS the room as my eyes open. I stretch and realize I'm covered with a blanket but alone on the couch. A glance around the room confirms what I already know, Max is gone. He must have covered me before he left. The simple gesture makes me smile. His absence this morning doesn't surprise me. Truthfully, I wasn't prepared to have an awkward morning after conversation anyway.

Another stretch reveals a delicious soreness between my legs. Max is every bit of the man I thought he would be. What I never expected was just how amazing he would make me feel. I've never been a multiple orgasm kind of girl, until Max. *Maybe it wasn't him. Maybe it was because it had been so long.* I laugh at my thoughts. It was most definitely him.

As I sit up, I grab my phone to check the time and see it's only seven. Max would be at work by now. I can't help but wonder what he thinks about last night. I dreamed he kissed me on the cheek before he left. That thought brings a laugh from me. Max isn't that kind of guy.

Even though it's early for me, I decide to get up and take a shower. As the water cascades down my body, the memory of Max's hands following the same path floods my mind. I think about his mouth as he kissed my skin, leaving fire raging with every touch. The tingle between my legs quickly becomes more than soreness. It becomes desire. More desire than I've ever had for anyone. *Stop it! It was one night!* The thoughts bring me back to the present.

My head drops to the wall of the shower as I remember Max's words. *"I can't promise you more than tonight. I'm not in a good place right now."* He didn't completely close the door to a repeat, but I know he meant to. How did I let this happen? *You didn't let it happen, you instigated it.*

Tears fall as I realize I *did* do this to myself. I wanted him and set the stage for what would happen. It was what I wanted, what I still want, and I got just what I asked for. Now I have to deal with the fact it probably ruined all other men for me. I knew it would before it ever happened, but I pursued him anyway.

There are so many reasons Max and I can never be together. His resistance is just one of them. His feelings for my best friend is another, but my past is the biggest. I can't put anyone in the position of having to deal with my past and the chance it might put their lives in danger. Who would want to be with me long term once they found out about my baggage? Baggage that no one but Gemma knows about. Baggage that I can never share with a man.

I raise my face into the water. No more tears. I don't cry, I haven't in years. It doesn't do any good, so why waste the energy. I will not start again by crying over Max Greenwood. Last night was fabulous with great sex and memories that I'll carry with me. Max gave me what I've wanted for years, a night with him.

When my shower is done, I wrap myself in my pink fuzzy robe. It was a gift from Gemma and I spend way too much time in it. The soft material against my skin comforts me. I wander to my kitchen and make a cup of coffee. Back in the living room, I stop in front of my couch. It is the only piece of furniture to sit on in the room and I'll never look at it again without the memory of the wickedly wonderful things Max did to me on it. Without another choice of place to sit, I plop down on the couch. Once settled and comfy, my thoughts drift to the first day I met Max.

The door to the salon opens and I lock to see who it is. Probably a walk-in, I think. In comes the most handsome guy I have ever seen. I freeze and watch him enter the room. He is over six feet tall with sandy colored hair. It's a little on the long side, sticking out from under the cap on his head. He strolls in like he owns the place, a commanding presence that usually makes me uncomfortable. For some reason, he doesn't elicit the same reaction I normally feel with confident men, all I feel is attraction.

He glances at me and I see the most glorious green eyes. He gives me a quick smile that takes my breath away before he continues to Gemma's station where she greets him with a hug. He says something quietly to her and she laughs. I find myself wishing it was my ear he was whispering in. Gemma turns my way and I chastise myself for that thought.

"Hey, Tiba. This is Max," Gemma tells me. Max.

This is the man she has told me so much about. The man who is her ex-husband but best friend.

"Hello, Tiba. It's good to finally meet you. Gem talks about you non-stop." The man says as he extends his hand to me. I reach out and shake his hand. As soon as our hands connect, sparks fly through my hand, up my arm. I look in his eyes to see if he felt the same thing and see nothing to indicate he did.

"Gemma talks about you too."

Gemma and I haven't worked together for long, but we have become close quickly. She has told me all about the relationship between her and Max. It's a relationship I still don't understand. With my past, I don't see how anyone can be best friends with their ex.

Gemma and Max chat with me for a few more minutes. I can't tear my eyes away from him. He is simply the most gorgeous man I have ever seen. Almost too pretty to be a man. And built like a rock. I know he works in construction, but he must work out. As the two leave the salon together, I know I want this man. I also know he is a man I can never have.

Nothing has changed since that day. I still can't have Max. I say nothing has changed, but one thing has, understanding the relationship between Gemma and Max. Gemma does only love him as a friend. Their marriage was not what she has with Raef.

The only problem is that Max loves Gemma. He told her as much right before the wedding. I know this, yet I just had sex with the man, letting my wants and desires take the forefront. I know better than to do that. I gave up the ability to think of myself first many years ago.

Before I can let my thoughts drift back to

that time in my life, my phone rings. Seeing it's Gemma, I debate whether to answer, but decide I will. Gemma doesn't call this early unless she needs something.

"Hey, girlie," I answer, trying to sound as normal as possible. The last thing I need is to tell Gemma what went on here last night.

"Hey, Tiba! Kathleen called this morning and invited us all for dinner tonight. She's having a little celebration for Jack's birthday." Gemma's excitement is evident. Could the timing be any worse? I can't go to Max's parents' house tonight. I can't face him this soon.

"Umm, I have a lot of clients today and might have to work late. I better skip this one."

"Nope, we won't take no for an answer. Kathleen wants you there. We'll pick you up at six. If you run behind, call me and I'll come in and help you with your clients."

"Yeah, whatever." My answer relays no enthusiasm. That doesn't stop Gemma.

"Get in a better mood! We'll have fun tonight. Got to go. Time to get Charley's breakfast ready." And just like that she's gone. Gemma is so full of energy since Raef has been back in her life.

Sighing, I put the phone down. I shouldn't have answered that call, but Gemma would have just shown up at the shop if I didn't answer. She wouldn't let me avoid her. And she is right, I should go for Jack's birthday. Jack and Kathleen are both very good to me and I am grateful for it. With no relationship with my parents, it's nice to have a family that loves me. I lean my head back on the couch and close my eyes.

Why did it have to be tonight? The thought runs through my mind like a song on repeat. Max and I might as well face the music and get this first time over with. It will be awkward, but it will happen sooner or later. It might as well be sooner.

With my coffee finished, I get ready for my day. I choose a favorite pair of heels and think of Max wanting me to keep my heels on last night. Shoes are my guilty pleasure but tonight these will be my armor. With them on my feet and a smile on my face, I'll face Max and let him know I accept last night on his terms.

I do, don't I?

Chapter 5

MAX

TODAY HAS BEEN A VERY long one. After my talk with Jerry, I called everyone at the job together for an impromptu meeting We had a good talk and I assured them that I will in fact *get my shit together*. I felt good after and worked my butt off at the site. Since Dad turned the company over to me, most days I don't have time to get out there and get my hands dirty. Days like today, when I can jump in and work on the building make me feel more alive. Construction is in my blood and I love the physical part of the work.

While putting up my tools, my phone rings. When I grab it out of my pocket, I see the call is from Mom. I answer because if I don't, she will call back over and over until I do.

"Hey, Mom. What's up?"

"Just your dad's birthday. Or did you forget?"

"Shit! I did forget!" I rub my hand on my forehead. How in the world did I forget my own father's birthday? *Tiba.* The one word drifts through my mind. I lean my head back and look at the sky.

"Language, Max. Don't stress too much. He's been busy with the horses today." Mom pauses, and

I breathe a small sigh of relief. "I'm having a cake out here tonight for him. You'll be here for dinner." Mom leaves no room for a no in this conversation.

"Yes, Mom. I'll be there. Just finished up here at the job. I'll head out as soon as I clean up. Love you." Mom responds with her 'love you' and we end the call. That's one thing I can always count on with my parents. They make sure I know they love me and I do the same for them, even though I can obviously forget a birthday.

I finish up and lock the gate at the job site. When I get in my truck, I realize I don't have a gift for my father. I glance at my watch and know I don't have time to run back into to town after I shower, but I know one thing he would love so I make a quick call to a friend. I'm pretty sure Dad will like my plan.

It doesn't take long to get a shower and dress for the evening. My family is down-to-earth, so we don't do fancy dinners. Just blue jeans and a t-shirt. As I stretch the shirt across my chest, I have a fleeting memory of Tiba's hands there. All day the thoughts of her hands on my body have invaded my thoughts. The more I thought of her, the harder I worked in hopes the thoughts would drift away. They didn't.

I grab my keys and head out to the farm. The entire drive is plagued with thoughts of Tiba. *Why can't I get this woman out of my head? It was great sex but that's all it was.* I tell myself this over and over. It was one night. Maybe I just need some rest.

When I pull into the farm, Raef's car is parked by mom's. I should have known they would be here. I'll have to deal with their happy little family all night. Oh well, this morning I decided that today was the day I take my life back. This will just be another step in that direction. Gemma is Raef's, not mine. She never really was mine. The thought that usually drives a stake in my heart doesn't seem to have that affect tonight. I wait for the pain to hit but it doesn't. Interesting. Hopping out of the truck, I head to the house. Charley meets me at the door.

"Uncle Max! Uncle Max! I've missed you so much!" Charley jumps up and down at my feet. I scoop her up and she wraps her little arms around my neck.

"I missed you too, Munchkin." I give her a kiss on the cheek and walk into the house, still holding her.

The first thing I see when I get through the door is the last person I expected to see today. Tiba stands in the kitchen next to Mom, laughing while she helps cook. Time freezes. Charley rattles in my ear but I don't hear it. The only thing that has my attention is Tiba. She looks so ravishing. She has on a burgundy dress that makes her skin color even more beautiful. My eyes drift to her feet and I see the heels. Heels like the ones that were wrapped around my back less than 24 hours ago.

Charley grabs my face to get my attention. I look at her little face next to mine and see it scrunched in pure frustration. She puts her tiny hands on her hips even though she sits in my arms.

"You're not listenin' to me, Uncle Max!" Charley tells me in her four-year old exasperation.

"I'm sorry, Munchkin. What were you saying?"

"I was sayin'," Charley says waving her hands

toward the kitchen, "that Auntie T came with us. We're gonna' eat cake for Papa's birthday!"

"I see that and yes we are." By this time, we are in the kitchen and I greet Mom with a kiss on the cheek. "Hey, Mom."

Tiba's eyes jerk to mine when she hears my voice. She gives me a weak smile and a small wave. I am lost in her gorgeous brown eyes and my brain can't seem to focus a single thought. Charley makes sure I don't stay lost for long.

"Uncle Max! You're not listenin' again!" Charley berates me. Mom and Tiba both laugh as I beg forgiveness from Charley.

Tiba's cheeks turn pink and she turns back to the salad she is preparing. Mom grabs me for a hug after I put Charley down.

"Son, that little one has you wrapped."

"I know, Mom. She does. Where's Dad?"

"He's out at the barn showing Raef and Gemma his new horse." Mom smiles like she always does when she talks about my dad, a smile that lights up her entire face. They have set the relationship bar very high.

"Think I'll head out there then." I walk over to the salad bowl in front of Tiba and grab a cherry tomato out of it. I lean over when I do so I can whisper in her ear without Mom noticing. "Nice shoes." With a smile, I pop the tomato in my mouth and leave Tiba with her mouth open.

"Happy birthday, Dad," I greet my father inside the barn. "Hey Raef, hey Gem." Again, I wait for the burn of pain I usually feel when I see these two. And again, it's not there.

Raef shakes my hand and Gemma gives me a

hug before my father grabs me in a bear hug. We are huggers in my family, even the men.

"Glad to see you, son. You haven't been out here in a while." Dad just had to throw that out there. A glance toward Raef and Gemma catches them as they squirm. Gemma twists her hands like she always does when she is nervous. Raef notices and takes one of her hands in his. I smile at his protectiveness.

"Sorry, Dad. It's been a strange few weeks, but things are back on track." I nod in the direction of Raef and Gemma to try to let them know I am okay with them. They both seem to let out breaths I didn't realize they were holding. They return the gesture with smiles as if they understand the implications of my action.

"Jack, I think Gemma and I are going to head back in to see if we can help Kathleen. Beautiful new addition to your horse family. I know you'll enjoy him." Raef leads Gemma out of the barn as Dad thanks him.

"So, son. What's been up with you? You never stay away this long." Dad's a man of few words and always gets straight to the point.

"It's been rough, Dad. I didn't handle Raef and Gemma's marriage too well. I didn't want to run into them here, but more than that, I didn't want you to see me in the shape I was in." I run my hand through my hair as I think about how out of control I've been.

"Jerry told me things haven't been good. You know you can talk to me anytime, son. I love Gemma, but you're still my son. I'm here for you, too." Dad grips my shoulder with his hand.

"I know, Dad. I didn't want to talk to anyone. I wanted to wallow in my misery. And that's what I did. I drank too much and even put my relationship with some of the guys at work at risk. Basically, I screwed up. Jerry called me out on it this morning and I'm back on track." I look at Dad and hope I don't see disappointment. I don't. Dad is nothing if not supportive.

"You looked like it didn't bother you too much a few minutes ago. You handled seeing them well."

"You know what? It's weird. The pain that usually is there when I think of Gemma isn't there tonight. It didn't bother me to see them together. In fact, I'm happy for them." As I say the words, I realize I really am happy for them. Gemma and Raef love each other. Gemma deserves to be happy. I smile at my father. "I really mean that, too. I'm happy that Gemma is happy."

Dad smiles back at me and pulls me into another hug. Did I mention we are huggers? He beams at me after we separate.

"You know what that is, son? That's progress. I don't know what happened to bring on this change, but I'm proud of you. Gemma is happy, and I want you to be too. I think you are headed that way." Dad drops his hand from my shoulder where it had remained. "Let's head in and see if dinner is ready."

Tiba. The name floats into my mind. *Tiba is what happened.* The thought shocks me. Is it true? Is Tiba what has caused this change in me? Did she make the pain go away? A smile forms when I realize she just might be the reason. I don't know if I'm ready for a relationship, but if she brought on this big of a change after one night, I think I may be ready to explore where this could go. I follow my father out of the barn with the biggest smile I've had in a long time.

Chapter 6

TIBA

NICE SHOES. THE WORDS ECHO in my mind. I can't believe Max said that to me in his mom's kitchen. And he smiled while he said it. What did he mean? I pull myself together before Kathleen notices something is off with me. It's not the time for her to ask questions. I finish the salad and chat with Kathleen, but I can't get those two words to go away. *Nice shoes.* That comment makes me wonder about my choice of footwear. These heels certainly don't feel much like armor right now. More like a chink in any armor I may have tried to put up.

The front door opens and I look over my shoulder to see Raef and Gemma. They hold hands and chat as they come to the kitchen. Watching them, I think of what a wonderful couple they are. I want that. I want what they have. Shaking my head, I turn back to the salad. I can never have that. I'm on my own. That's my choice. I won't bring someone into the nightmare of the life I left behind.

"Gemma, do you mind setting the table?" Kathleen asks, bringing me out of my thoughts. "Don't mind at all! Raef will help."

Raef follows her to get the dishes without any complaints. Raef is a wealthy man, the owner of an international company, yet he happily helps his wife set the table. I am so happy my friend has the love of her life.

The door opens again, and Jack and Max come in. My breath catches when I see Max. That man always takes my breath away. His eyes meet mine and he smiles from ear-to-ear. I tilt my head in shock. Max looks happy, something I haven't seen in months. I like it and I like that it seems to be directed at me. As much as I don't want to, I break my eyes away from his and take the salad to the table.

Max walks by me as I bring more food to the table. He casually leans over as he passes and whispers, "You look beautiful." He reaches out to steady me when I stumble. As soon as his hands touch me, my body tingles. I jerk my head toward him.

"Careful, don't trip with the food." Max moves his hands away and I feel the loss of his touch. My voice won't work, so I just nod and put the plate on the table.

Everyone finds a seat around the table and the chatter begins. Charley leads the conversation as usual. Everyone laughs at her stories while I steal glances over to Max when I can. We are seated by each other as usual with Raef and Gemma on the other side of the table. Max smiles and talks like he did before Raef came into the picture. I find myself wondering what happened. Just last night, the man was a mess. Now he seems happy as a lark.

Suddenly I feel a hand on my thigh. I jump and drop my fork on the plate. The clatter of the metal hitting the porcelain causes everyone to stop talking and turn my way. I feel heat creep up my cheeks.

"You okay, Auntie T?" Charley asks.

"I'm fine." It comes out as a mutter. All eyes are on me. A peek to the side finds Max with a huge grin on his face. He knows exactly why I jumped. I glare at him, but he just gives me a smirk. His hand begins to move on my thigh. I can't believe he is doing this here.

"Are you sure? You look funny!" Charley says with her nose scrunched.

"Charley!" Gemma exclaims with embarrassment. Raef covers his mouth with his hand as he laughs. Jack and Kathleen look down at their plates as they fight their own laughter. I look back at Max and he chuckles.

"Yeah, T. You sure you're okay?" Max asks. He just called me T. He has never done that before. I glare at him again before I look around to see if anyone else notices. Gemma does and looks from Max to me with questions in her eyes. Raef is all but choking on his laughter. Suddenly I'm the center of attention for the family meal. The heat on my face tells me that I'm blood red right now. My dark skin can't even hide it. It's time to get these people focused on something else. I decide Charley is the way to do that.

"I'm fine, Charley. What did you do today at the sitter's house?" Redirection at its finest and Charley jumps on it. My focus is back on my plate while Charley talks. Max chuckles quietly next to me, his hand still on my leg.

After dinner, we enjoy a cake for Jack's birthday.

Kathleen gives him a new saddle along with a few new shirts for his gifts. Raef and Gemma give him a framed photo of Charley from the wedding for his office in the barn. Charley climbs onto his lap while he opens a card she made for him. Of course, that is the best present because Charley made it all by herself. Jack promises it will go in his office also.

I slip the card I purchased for Jack across the table. Surprise registers in his face as he accepts it. He nods in appreciation and opens it. The card says things I can't vocalize to him, but I want to make sure he knows just how much he means to me. With no father in my life, Jack has become a father-figure. I included a gift card to the local sporting goods store. After all, what do you get a man like Jack? He can buy anything he wants for himself.

Jack looks up from the card. His eyes glisten with unshed tears. My own eyes feel like they may shed a tear any minute.

"Thank you, Tiba. This means a lot to me. You are a part of this family and we love you." Jack glances at the gift card. "You didn't have to get me a gift, but thanks! I can already think of a thing or two to spend this on." He gives me a big smile and a wink.

Max's hand finds my leg again, giving it a squeeze. My eyes move to his and I see respect and admiration in them. He breaks our gaze and looks back to his father.

"Dad, I couldn't wrap my gift for you. I'm taking you on a weekend deep sea fishing trip. We just have to pick a weekend."

Jack's eyes light up with excitement.

"Well, thank you, Max! That sounds wonderful. You know how much I enjoy fishing." Jack looks back at me. "I've just come up with something else to buy with this gift card." Everyone laughs at his joke.

We move to the living room and chat for another hour or so. Charley falls asleep in Jack's lap and he seems perfectly content to hold her while she sleeps. Raef looks at his watch and reaches for Gemma's hand.

"Folks, it's time to get my little family home for the night." Raef and Gemma stand, and I follow suit since I rode with them. Raef eases Charley into his arms without waking her.

While Raef gets Charley in her booster seat, Gemma and I say our goodbyes to Jack and Kathleen. Just as I open the back door of Gemma's vehicle, Max appears with a hand on my arm.

"Let me take you home," Max says as he eases me away from the door. I quickly glance around to make sure no one is watching us.

"No, I don't want to raise suspicions. We've already attracted enough attention with that stunt you pulled at dinner. What were you thinking?"

Max gives me a low chuckle. "That was all you, sweetheart. You are the one who almost jumped out of the chair."

"You are the one who grabbed my leg!" I answer indignantly. "Even Charley noticed something was up."

Max leans over closer to me. "I just felt the need to touch you. There was no grabbing. More like massaging." His lips are almost on mine. "How about that ride home?" His words are spoken softly against my skin. I so want to kiss him right now. It's probably a mistake, but I want to ride home with him. I want a repeat of last night.

"Okay. I'll ride with you, but you better come up with some good excuse. I don't want Raef and Gemma asking questions."

"You've got it." Max puts his keys in my hand. "Go ahead and get in the truck. I'll go tell them."

Max jogs back to the group. He tells them something and Gemma nods. Raef shakes his hand and says something back to him. Unfortunately, they are too far away for me to hear what they are saying. Gemma looks my way, but since I don't want her to make eye contact with me right now, I make my trek to the passenger side of Max's truck. With the door open, I begin to try to get myself inside without having my dress wind up over my head. Why do men want such big trucks? They sure don't make it easy for a woman in a dress and heels. By the time I make it inside, Max is back.

"Sure wish I had gotten back here sooner. Would've loved to see you climb up there in those shoes." Max runs his hand down my leg to my ankle, leaving shivers in his wake. "Yes, indeed. I would've enjoyed that."

"Shut up and get in, big guy." I feel the heat in my cheeks. Max laughs but shuts the door. After he makes it to his side and gets in the truck, I have to know what he told Gemma and Raef. "So, what excuse did you use for taking me home?"

"I told them that we were going home to have hot sex," Max replies without changing his expression. My mouth drops open and I can't respond. He glances over and sees the look on my face and bursts into laughter. "I told them I would take you home so they could get Charley home and in bed. That look on your face just then was priceless though."

Relief floods through me and I level Max with a glare. Such a jokester. I almost passed out when he said he had told them we were going to have sex, but I can't help but wonder if that's what we are about to do. And I have to admit I wouldn't mind it too much at all.

C. KAYE

Chapter 7

MAX

THE LOOK ON TIBA'S FACE was one I won't soon forget. It was a cross between shock, fear, and anger. Now, I am the recipient of a glare that I deserve. I know she doesn't mean it though because I can see the desire in her eyes. It's the direct opposite of what she is attempting to portray.

"Cat got your tongue over there?" I can't help but prod her a little. She is so much fun to play with.

"Not at all. I felt like that little stunt you just pulled didn't deserve a response." Tiba tries to maintain a haughty expression. Her mouth gives her away with her lips pinched tightly trying to hold in a smile.

"You have to admit it was pretty funny. That look on your face." I shake my head and laugh. "That's a look I'll remember for quite some time."

A small giggle comes from Tiba and I steal a glance her way. Her smile has broken through and it's dazzling. The sight of it makes my chest feel funny. Why do I always feel like something is wrong with me when I am around this sexy woman?

"Okay, okay. It was funny. But it almost gave me

a heart attack."

"Sorry about that. I just couldn't resist." Another glance her way and I catch her staring at me. "I wouldn't mind it happening though. The sex part that is." Tiba's eyes sparkle and her cheeks turn a light shade of pink. She doesn't look away, just stands her ground.

"Hmmm. I don't know. We tried that last night and it wasn't very good. Not sure I want a repeat of that."

Slamming on the brakes of my truck, I pull us to the side of the road. I can't believe she just said that. Last night was great and she knows it. She enjoyed it. Frustration creeps up the back of my neck. I throw the truck in park and turn to Tiba, ready to make her remember how good last night was. She holds her stomach in fits of laughter. I open my mouth to say something but close it again. She got me. I throw my head back and join the hilarity of the moment.

"Paybacks a bitch, big guy. That's what you get for what you said earlier. I wish *you* could've seen *your* face. You were about to go all alpha male on me."

"I was ready to remind you just how good last night was for *both* of us. I thought you had amnesia or something."

"No amnesia. I remember." Tiba's chuckles are gone and her voice is husky. Her alluring eyes are dark with desire. The look she gives me has my jeans tightening. Damn this girl can make me hard without even trying.

Leaning over the console, I put my hand on the back of her neck and pull her in for a kiss. I keep it short and chaste so we can make it home. If I let myself kiss her any deeper, I'll take her right here on the side of the road. That wouldn't be smart for either of us. Her lips are still close to mine when I pull back. They tempt me, but I resist. Instead, I run my thumb over them.

"I've wanted to do that all night," I say as Tiba slips her tongue between her lips and lightly licks my thumb as it caresses her bottom lip. My erection strains against the denim. "Keep that up and we won't make it home."

Tiba chuckles as she leans back in her seat, moving away from my lingering hand. I use my other hand to adjust myself, seeking a little relief. Out of the corner of my eye, I see her watching me. I reach for her hand and lay it on top of my erection. "That's what you do to me," I tell her as I put the truck in drive. One more look at her beautiful smile and I pull back onto the road. She surprises me and leaves her hand in my lap.

I drive faster than I should to get to Tiba's apartment. She has the keycard ready for the gate when we arrive. I make quick work of finding a parking place, jump out of the truck, and circle around to her side to find her door already open. She stands on the running boards looking all kinds of sexy. Holding her by her waist, I pull her to me and let her body slide down mine until she stands on the ground. Her dress bunches between us and is almost high enough to reveal just what I want to see. Since I don't want anyone else to see, I back away an inch and let the material fall back around her legs.

My hands glide up her body to tilt her face

upward. My lips find hers in a kiss that is nowhere near chaste this time. My tongue slips in her mouth and duels with hers while her hands tightly grip my shirt.

Breathless, I grudgingly pull my lips from Tiba's. My hands drift to her shoulders. Her lips remain parted and her eyes hooded. The look is insanely sexy and almost has me diving back in for more. A car pulls through the apartment gates and reminds me where we are.

"Can I come inside?" The thought she might say no pops in my mind. I caress her shoulders while I await her answer. I'm so happy to see a nod and smile come from her. Taking her hand in mine, I breathe a sigh of relief. She looks down at our joined hands as we walk to the apartment.

Tiba finds her keys in her purse quickly this time and unlocks the apartment. We are barely through the door when I grab her waist from behind and pull her body against mine. I dip my head and my lips find her neck. She tilts her head slightly and I trail kisses until I nip at her ear. That gets a moan from her that goes straight to my groin. Turning her to face me, I immediately devour her lips. Her hands rest against my hips while mine hold her body tightly to me. I tear myself away from her long enough to mutter the word "bedroom."

With a smirk, Tiba tips her head to the side and points toward a door on the opposite side of the room. I grab her sexy ass in my hands, lifting her in the air as her legs wrap around my body. My mouth finds hers again and we kiss greedily as we cover the short distance to the bedroom. Her skirt is bunched around her waist and I realize that she isn't wearing anything underneath.

"Damn. It's a good thing I didn't know you were bare under there. We may not have made it back to the apartment before I had to have you." I flick on the light switch to find the bed in the tiny room. Loving the feel of her legs around me and not wanting to break that connection, we fall together onto the bed.

Tiba's hands venture under my shirt, finding my skin. Her fingertips burn a path along my back. Our kiss deepens as I fight to keep control. I want to be inside her so badly, but I want to taste every inch of her first. I finally break away to remove her skirt and top. It only takes a moment and I'm rewarded with the sight of her seductive body before me in nothing but her heels. I can't pull my gaze away from her as I languidly move my hands along her body. There are a few scars on her stomach that I didn't see last night and move my finger across them. I want to ask what happened, but I don't want to ruin the mood, so I let it go for now.

Sitting up for a moment, I pull my shirt off and lay back beside Tiba. She turns her head toward me and I kiss her gently. I trail kisses down her neck and chest. Her breasts call to me and I can no longer resist. With one nipple in my mouth, I tweak the other with my fingers. Her breaths come faster and she squirms beneath me. Unhurriedly, I move back and forth between her breasts until I can take it no more. There is another destination in my mind. I want to taste this beautiful imp.

My tongue trails down her stomach. She doesn't expect it and her body jumps. I smile at the reaction but continue all the way to her center. Raising myself off her slightly, I gently part her legs. One hand holds myself up and the other moves as light as feathers along the inside of both legs. Before I move to taste her, I glance to see her sexy eyes as she watches me. She places one hand on her stomach and the other on the side of my face.

"I have wanted to taste you all night." My voice is raspy with desire. "I don't know what you've done to me, but I can't stop thinking about you."

"Just working some magic." Tiba smirks. That smirk is so hot.

Growling in response, I lower my head to feast on her. One swipe of my tongue and she gasps. She tastes so damn good, I could gasp too. I can tell she's already close, and it won't take long to send her over the edge. As much as I want to draw this out, I want to give her pleasure even more. I slip one finger inside her, seeking the spot that makes her come alive. My tongue continues its exploration while I slip in a second finger. She's so tight around them and when I curve my fingers, I find just what I was looking for. The combination of the stroke of my fingers and the steady persistence of my tongue has her on the edge. The feel of her tightening around my fingers tells me she is there. One more swipe of my tongue and she explodes, gripping my hair as she does. My tongue stays on her and brings her back down from the high before I quickly remove my jeans.

Once I have the condom out of my pocket, Tiba takes it from my hand. She slowly rolls it on my length and it's all I can do to keep from letting go just from the feel of her small fingers on me. I hold my breath until she finishes and moves me to her entrance. Her eyes find mine and the gold flecks in them sparkle. I ease into her and her eyes roll back into her head. We both moan as I move gently until I have worked my way fully into her. Pausing, I gaze down at her. Her wild hair is all over the pillow, eyes are closed, and mouth parted as she pants with desire. When I touch her cheek with the back of my hand, her eyes flutter open. I begin to move inside her very, very slowly with our eyes locked on each other.

Tiba's hands grip my hips as I begin to move faster. I am so close, and I know I won't be able to last long. I seek out her lips and kiss her with all the passion I feel. My pace quickens as I near the finish line. I tear my lips from hers.

"I'm close. Come with me, Tiba." Her gaze is glued to mine and her breaths quicken as does my pace.

My hips take on a life of their own and move furiously. Tiba's hands are so tight on me and I feel her nails dig into my sides. I raise myself slightly and shift her below me for a different angle. As the build of my orgasm reaches its height, I reach between us to make sure she is with me. Just as I do, I come with a roar. I shout her name as she follows me with her own orgasm. Hers seems to prolong my own to a point I have never felt before. Neither of us move for several moments as we both try to come back to our senses.

"Wow," I say as I finally slide out of her and roll to my side. "That was amazing." I kiss the tip of her nose before I sit up to remove the condom.

"It was pretty amazing."

"I need to get rid of this." I point to the condom.

I kiss her before I stand and head to the bathroom. I look over my shoulder at her on top of the bed, still in her heels. "Why don't you take those sexy shoes off . . . I'll be right back."

Before I head back into the bedroom, I take a long look in the mirror. The reflection I see is not the same man I've seen for the last several weeks. That man was full of despair and heartache. The man I see right now looks happy. I had forgotten what being happy felt like and it feels pretty damn good.

Smiling at myself, I run my fingers through my hair. Two days ago, I was a shell of a man, miserable and angry. Two nights with Tiba and I'm a whole new me. I don't know where this thing with us is going, but I am definitely interested in finding out.

Chapter 8

TIBA

AMAZING. ONE SIMPLE LITTLE WORD that describes so much more than the sex we just had. It describes everything to do with Max Greenwood. If only I could tell him that. But, I can't. For many reasons. He is in love with my best friend. I shouldn't even be having sex with him for that reason alone. I just can't seem to control myself when he is around. Never would I have thought I would have the chance to be with him one time, much less two. This has to be the last time though. There is heartbreak on the horizon for me if I let this continue. I can never compete with Gemma where Max is concerned. Even if I could, he deserves more of a life than I would be able to give him. My past has marked my future.

The door to the bathroom opens and I quickly cover myself with the comforter. I don't know what to expect now. Will it be awkward conversation? Will Max just get dressed and leave? I probably should have gotten dressed while he was in the bathroom, but I just didn't have it in me. The part of me that has been in love with him for years wants him to stay, but the wise part of me knows he should leave. As the internal struggle inside me continues, I feel the bed dip.

"You look deep in thought." Max eases under the covers and pulls me to him. My heart wins over my head and I let him cuddle me into his side, my head on his arm.

"Just thinking about some things."

"You're not supposed to be thinking after great sex." Max tilts my face toward his and he kisses me so softly I wonder if his lips actually touched mine. "Now is the time to relax and talk about how long we have to wait before we do that again."

I can't help but smile at Max. He looks so sincere. Even more, he looks happy. I am so used to the scowl on his face, it shocks me to see him smile. And even more, to smile at me. I want to feel happy too—and I do when I am with him. At least, when I am not thinking about how this might be the last time I'll be with him.

"Well, big guy, I think that all depends on you and how soon you can be ready." I poke him in the chest playfully.

"If that's all we are waiting on then it won't be long." Max grips my hip and pulls me against his already growing erection.

"Okay, okay. I was joking. After last night and then tonight, I don't know if I'm ready again." Laughing, I push him away. "It's been a while and you aren't exactly a small man."

"That's right, missy. I am a *big* guy in every way." Max pulls me back against him tightly. He chuckles as he kisses me. "I guess I'll give you a break for a few hours."

My head rests on Max's arm. My fingers trail circles on his chest. As happy as I am in the moment, I know I can't just let it go on. We need to talk. We are friends and I can't afford to let sex ruin that friendship.

"What are we doing here, Max?" I say softly, still tracing the circles on his skin.

"I think this is what they call cuddling or something like that."

I pull away just enough where I can look at him. He smiles down to me, his green eyes sparkle with mischief.

"Seriously, though. We are friends. We share the same friends. What are we doing in bed together, not once but twice?"

Max drops the smile and seems to concentrate on the question. His fingers lightly slide up and down my back. It is terribly distracting for me.

"Well, I guess we moved from friends to lovers sometime last night." He gazes into my eyes as he awaits my response.

"But this can't ruin our friendship. Sex can't ruin our friendship."

"I don't think it's ruining anything. Why do you think it is?"

"If it continues, it will. There is no way this can end well."

"I'll be honest. I don't know where this is going but I have enjoyed the last two nights with you more than anything in a very long time." Max tilts my head and kisses me again.

"We agreed last night that this was a one-time thing and now here we are again. We can't keep falling into bed with each other."

"Why not?" He gives that killer smile again. So

much sexier than a scowl. "I think we are doing pretty good in bed." He gets my trademark smirk in response for that. He touches my lips with his thumb and chuckles. "That is one sexy smirk you have."

"Sexy wasn't what I was going for." We need to get back to the subject at hand. "Max, I don't do relationships and last night you admitted you aren't in a good place."

"I was in a good place a few minutes ago." He grinds his hips into mine. "When I was inside you."

"Oh, my goodness. Do you have a one-track mind?" I laugh.

"Around you, I think I do." He kisses me again. "I think you need to lighten up a little bit and let's just see where this goes."

"I don't do relationships." Even though my words are saying one thing, I let him continue to kiss me.

"We won't call it a relationship then." Max rolls us over to where he is on top of me again. He kisses me more deeply and I feel his erection growing. When he kisses me like this, my brain ceases to function. Breathlessly, I pull back.

"Okay. But please don't tell anyone about this, or us, or whatever it is we're doing." Dark green eyes bore into mine. Max's brow draws into a frown, almost like the scowl I'm used to seeing. I try to turn my eyes away, but he stops me.

"For now, this will be our little secret." Max's hand lightly rubs my cheek. "Not sure why, but I won't argue since we don't know where this will wind up."

My hands wrap around his neck and pull him down. I kiss him with everything I have. I can do this. I can be his sexual release for a little while. We can make more memories for me to have when he moves on. As much as I want to believe that he thinks this could be more, I know I can't give him a relationship. There is no future with me, so why mess around with the present? I guess I am selfish and want a little piece of him.

Max rolls over and reaches into the pocket of his jeans. He comes back with another condom and quickly has it on. He pulls me on top of him and slides back into me. I throw my head back in ecstasy and decide that now is definitely not the time to think about anything other than this moment.

Chapter 9

MAX

I AWAKEN TO A TINY BROWN body wrapped around mine. Tiba's crazy hair tickles my nose. I move my head slightly away from her curls but not enough to wake her. She is peacefully sleeping with her head on my arm. She has one arm thrown over my side and her leg over my legs. Normally, I would feel trapped waking up to a woman like this, but I don't feel that at all. In fact, I want to stay and enjoy the moment.

Last night was nothing short of amazing. After the third time we orgasmed together, we both decided we better get a little bit of sleep. Never before have I experienced sex like I have with Tiba. I don't know what it means or even if I want to know what it means. I just know I enjoy being with her.

Our conversation last night was odd. Tiba was very adamant about not doing relationships. I don't know if a relationship is what I want or not. Two days ago, I would have said it definitely was not what I wanted. At that time, all I could think about was losing Gemma. Or at least that is what I thought. Mixed in with those thoughts was always a kiss in a barn. A kiss shared with Tiba. A kiss that burned into my soul. A kiss that made me finally start to see that maybe my mom has been right all along, and I don't love Gemma the way I thought I did.

A glance at the clock tells me that my mind has wandered for longer than I thought. I need to get up and get to work. I have to run by my house since I don't have any work clothes with me. Today is one of those days I love where I get to be on the jobsite and be hands on. Even that thought doesn't make me want to leave this warm body attached to mine.

Not wanting to disappear again like I did yesterday morning, I gently kiss Tiba. She stirs but doesn't awaken. I kiss her a little harder. Her eyes fly open and there is a look of fear in them. I pull back quickly, not having intended to frighten her.

"Hey, it's just me." I caress her shoulder and down her arm. She calms and quickly turns her face from mine.

"Um, sorry. Just not used to waking up with someone."

"No problem. I probably shouldn't have kissed you to wake you up." I turn her face back toward mine. "But, now that you are awake, I will kiss you again." And that is what I do. I kiss her. This time, she relaxes and kisses me back. Much too soon, I have to break away.

"I hate to leave, but I have to run by the house and then get to work."

"What time is it?"

"It's 5:30." Tiba groans when she hears the time. "I need to be to the job by 6:30, so I am already pushing it."

"Go." She throws a pillow at me. "Let me go back to sleep."

"Yes, ma'am." I chuckle. After another quick kiss, I get out of bed. I throw on my clothes and glance back one last time at her. She has fallen back asleep and I can't help but smile. She has changed my attitude about life without even knowing it.

I quietly close the bedroom door as I leave. The pictures on the wall over the couch catch my attention. Tiba has a huge amount of talent with a camera. It's amazing that she hides it from the world. She could make a fortune selling her photos. Shaking my head at the senselessness of it, I make sure I lock the door behind me as I exit the apartment.

The drive to my house is short, thank goodness. I run in, take a quick shower, and put on my work clothes before heading out. Thank goodness we are working on a building in town or I would be very late. The guys at work would enjoy that.

When I pull into the parking lot of the job, I see Jerry get out of his truck. I wave for him to wait on me while I park. I jump out of the truck and jog over to where he waits.

"Ya' look a lot better than yesterday, son." Jerry pats me on the back in greeting.

"I feel a lot better. Thanks for giving me the kick in the ass I needed." Thoughts of Tiba flit through my mind and I smile. "You gave me the push I needed to get my act together."

"Whoa! Is that a smile? I thought ya' forgot how to."

"Ah, the jokester."

Jerry and I laugh as we enter the job site. I open

the small temporary office building while Jerry meanders to the building in progress. Greenwood Construction is working on a new medical building. It is right next to the local hospital and is one of the largest projects we have undertaken.

The magnitude of the job has been a challenge for our company and one my father was concerned about. Once he turned the day-to-day operations of the business over to me, I was ready to move us into a different direction. I have known for some time we can compete with the big firms from the city that consistently take the larger jobs in our area. Dad pushed back when I decided to bid on this job but since he had put me in charge, he gave in. We won the bid easily because we have local labor and don't have the extra costs of bringing in workers. It wasn't just a good move for us, it was a good move for the community. We put more of our local part-timers to work full-time. Now I have to make sure we deliver the perfect building on time.

The next hour is spent going over the plans for the building. The hospital board had some changes they threw on us last week and the architect sent over the updated plans yesterday. From the looks of things, they didn't change anything we have already completed. That's good news.

Once I know what we are looking at, I call everyone at the site together for a brief meeting and point out the changes for the area we are working on today. When we all are on the same page, I jump in to work beside the others. This is my happy place. Being on the site with the guys. Well, guys and gals. This job has some female workers and they happen to be some of the best carpenters I have worked with.

After hours of good hard and sweaty work, we call it a day. I make sure to speak to every worker before they head home. With my bad attitude the last few weeks, I haven't focused on the morale of the employees. I want to turn that around and make sure they all know I have their backs and appreciate their work. As usual, Jerry is the last to leave. He stands to the side as I shake hands with the last of the guys and only approaches me when they are all out of the gate.

"Good work t'day, son. Glad to see ya' back in the saddle here. Job this big needs it."

"You're right, Jerry. Sorry I've been so aloof lately. It won't happen again. Dad entrusted this company to me and even though he didn't like it, he's backed me in taking on this project."

"He's proud of ya'. This job won't be any different. Just bigger." Jerry clasps my hand. "Wanna' get a drink with me?"

"Not tonight. I, um, have some things to work on." All I want to do is find Tiba and lose myself with her after a long day at the job. Jerry guffaws as I stumble on my words.

"Things to work on, boy? I know what ya' wanna' work on." With that he turns and leaves.

Shaking my head, I go back into the office. I guess I didn't do very good at convincing Jerry that I have work to do. The old man can see right through me. There are times I think he is as good as my father at that.

After looking at the new plans one more time in preparation for tomorrow, I pull out my phone.

It stays on silent when I'm working on a job site for safety purposes. The last thing I need is to be distracted by a ringing phone when I'm moving materials or swinging a hammer. I check my messages and see there is only one and it's from Gemma. That would have given me a jolt a few days ago, but interestingly, I feel no emotion remotely close to that. I click on the message to open it.

Gemma: *Hey. Call me when you get off work.*

Call Gemma. Again, a few days ago, I would have jumped on the phone immediately to dial her number. Today, do I really want to call her? I would rather call Tiba. But what if something is wrong with Charley? That's always a possibility and I would want to know. That little girl means the world to me. I decide I better make the call, so I do just that. The phone only rings once before Gemma answers.

"Hey, Max."

"Hey, Gem. I got your message. Everything okay? Charley okay?"

"Oh, yeah, everyone's fine. I was just wanted to check on Tiba. She was acting very odd last night, and she won't answer my calls today. Was she okay when you took her home?"

That explains the message and the reason for the call. Gemma is being a little nosy because she can't get in touch with Tiba. I want to chuckle but don't since I don't want to give anything away. Answering will have to be done carefully since Tiba and I agreed to keep this thing between us quiet.

"Hmm, I didn't notice anything. She seemed just fine when I left her." Not a lie. Tiba was fine when I left her *this morning*. In fact, she was *very* fine.

When I bring myself back to the present, I'm sitting in the chair on the phone grinning like a loon.

"It's just unusual for her not to answer my calls or texts. We talk every day and I feel like she is ignoring me today." Gemma sounds distraught.

"Maybe she just had a really busy day at the salon. You remember how it can get sometimes. I'm sure you will hear from her tonight." I'm going to need to make sure Tiba calls her tonight or Gemma will have more questions. This keeping quiet thing is harder than I thought it would be.

"I guess you're right. I just worry about her, you know. For so long we were both alone and now I have Raef. I just worry she feels even more alone than usual." Gemma has never been totally alone because she has my family, but she is so independent that she felt she was. Tiba is a different story. I don't know of any family in her life. In fact, I don't know much at all about her life other than what I see with Gemma and Charley. That's something I need to work on and now seems like a good opportunity without raising suspicion.

"You know you always have Mom and Dad. What's with Tiba, though? Now that you mention it, I've never heard her mention any family." *Smooth, Max.* Let's see if Gemma notices I am the one being nosy now.

"She doesn't talk to her family . . . " Gemma seems like she wants to say more but stops.

"Really? That's weird. Why doesn't she?"

"Not my story to tell." Gemma pauses. "Max, I need to go. Charley just yelled to tell me Raef is home. You know how she watches for him to come down the driveway every day since we moved into the new house."

"She's a cutie. Give her a hug for me."

"I will. Bye, Max." Gemma ends the call and I am left in silence.

My thoughts immediately turn back to Tiba. She doesn't talk to her family at all. What could have happened to keep her from them? I can't imagine not talking to my parents regularly. Truth be told, my dad is probably my best friend. I definitely trust him more than my other friends.

I decide to send a quick message to Tiba before I head home. I would really like to see her tonight, but I have no idea what her plans for the evening are.

Just got off work. Any plans tonight?

I stare at the message before pressing send. I don't want to sound too anxious to see her, do I? Why am I overthinking everything with her? *Just send the message, dumbass.* Listening to my head, I press send. I continue to watch the phone waiting on a response. After a few minutes, I wise up and realize Tiba isn't going to message me back right now. I can't believe I am sitting here watching a phone waiting on a message from a woman. What is she doing to me? Frustrated with myself, I lock the office and the fence gate. As I trudge across the parking lot, I berate myself for being a wuss about a girl. Didn't I just get over acting like that about Gemma? Tiba wants to keep us casual. That's my usual preference with a woman, so why does it bother me so much this time?

Maybe I should have taken Jerry up on his offer to get a drink. No, I am not turning back to that because I'm upset about a woman. I throw my truck into drive and hit the road to my house. I am going to go home, get a shower, and spend a quiet night at home. One where I make myself think about something other the beauty that has turned my world upside down in two days.

Chapter 10

TIBA

WHAT A DAY. I AM exhausted. Even so, I'm glad it has been busy so I could keep myself from thinking about Max all day. Having clients back-to-back kept me in conversation and out of my thoughts. I love to chat with the people who allow me to make them beautiful. But, standing all day does make my feet hurt sometimes and today is one of those times. I plop down on the couch in the salon to relax for a little bit before I go home.

This salon is like another home for me. I love being here. When I look around the room, I see a place that Gemma and I worked hard to make our own. Now, Gemma owns the place and I run it. I miss her being here with me every day, but I am happy for her. I sigh when I look at her station. She still comes in sometimes to help out when we are really busy, but most days her station stays empty. We hired another stylist to work with me and we get along great, but it's just not the same as having Gem with me.

Picking up my phone, I power it on. I usually never turn it off during the day, but today I did. Gemma may not be here with me, but not a day goes by that she doesn't call. I want so badly to talk to her about what is happening with Max. I'm afraid if I talk to her today, I might do just that.

When my phone powers up, it dings with messages and missed calls. Sure enough, almost all of them are from Gemma. There is one that isn't from her. It is from Max. My breath catches when I see it. My finger hovers over the message for a moment. Do I want to open it? I touch the message and it pops open.

Just got off work. Any plans tonight?

A simple message but one that means so much. Max messaged me when he got off work. My heart soars knowing he thought of me and appears to want to see me tonight. I hold the phone to my chest with both hands, close to my heart like a lovesick teenager. My head jumps into the act and brings me back to reality. I can't let this be more than it is.

There are things Max doesn't know about me. Things I don't plan on him ever knowing. Gemma is the only person in Granier who knows about my past. She knows the reason I don't have a relationship with my parents, my siblings. She knows why safety is very important to me. Most of all, she knows the one secret that means I can never be with Max the way I want to be.

The thoughts depress me. I don't normally let myself think about my past. Sitting here isn't going to make me feel any better so I get up and clean the salon. Once done, I grab my purse and lock up as I leave. When I get to my car, I check the back seat like I always do before I open the car door. It is a habit I can't seem to get out of. I make a quick look around my surroundings and then hop in the car.

On the short drive to my apartment, I can't get the text from Max off my mind. I haven't responded and I'm not sure how to. I want to tell him I have no plans and ask him to come over, but I know if I do, I will fall even deeper into this than I already am. I sure wish I could talk to Gemma about this. She would give me the best advice. It's not worth risking the friendship we all share to do that though. This thing with Max will end and we will all still be friends.

Sliding my card into the security system at my apartment complex, the large iron gate opens. I love my tiny little home. It is fenced in, gated, safe and secure. And, it is all mine. No one helped me get it, I did it all by myself. I pay my bills on my own and that means so much to me. I am totally independent. The thought cheers me a bit.

When I get in my apartment, my eyes are drawn to the photos that hang on my wall. They represent the one main joy in my life. I love to take pictures of anything and everything. Max asked why I don't sell my work. Little does he know that I want to so badly but doing so would open me up to the potential of so much misery in my life. Like everyone else in Granier, he doesn't know that I hide here from everyone I have ever known. Sharing the thing I enjoy the most could bring my past back into my life and I won't let that happen. I fought too hard to leave it behind.

My phone dings and drags my attention away from my photos. I see it is Gemma again.

Are you okay? Why haven't I heard from you today?

Call me! I'm worried!

The desperation of Gemma's text makes me giggle. Now that she stays home with Charley all day, she has way too much time on her hands. In her mind, she is probably worried sick about me just because I haven't talked to her today. I love that she cares about me so much, but she needs to lighten up a little. I need to suggest she find a hobby to fill her days. Since I don't want her to show up here to check on me, I hit her number to call her.

"Tiba! Are you okay? Why haven't you answered me calls?" Gemma doesn't even say hello, just jumps into the questions.

"Slow down, girlie. I'm fine. It was a crazy day at the shop and I had my phone turned off."

"You never turn your phone off? What's going on?"

"I had one client after another and didn't want to be bothered with it. Nothing is going on except I am dead on my feet. I'm ready for a hot bath and a glass of wine." I drop to the couch and put the phone on speaker so I can relax.

"Well, you had me worried about you all day. You were acting strange last night at Jack and Kathleen's. I thought you might be upset about something. You never ignore my calls." I chuckle at the sound of Gemma pouting. It's obvious where Charley gets it from.

"I'm sorry I worried you. I'm fine. You just need to remember that I still work at the salon every day. You know some days get wild over there."

"I know, I know. I'm sorry, too. Since I'm home all day, I tend to think everyone should be available when I want them to be. I need to work on that.

I'm still adjusting to this new life." Gemma sighs. "I love this, but I miss you. I miss adult conversation sometimes."

I had never thought about Gemma's situation that way. She has gone from being in a salon with adults all day long to being at home with a preschool child. She wouldn't have it any other way, but I can see where she comes from in the need for some adult time.

"You know it won't hurt Charley if you leave her with Alexis sometimes. I know Alexis probably misses her." Alexis had been Charley's sitter until recently.

"I know. I just feel guilty taking her to a sitter when I'm not working. She'll start pre-school soon and I'll have too much time on my hands then."

"Hang in there, girlie. You've had a lot of changes the last few months. How about you talk that sexy husband of yours into letting us have a girls' night? We'll grab a pizza or something."

"That sounds great!" Gemma's tone is chipper. "How about tomorrow night?"

"Works for me. I should finish up around six at the salon. Why don't you meet me there after Raef gets home?"

"Perfect. Thanks, Tiba. You always know how to make me feel better."

"I'm glad. See you tomorrow. I'm going to get that bath and wine now."

We end the call and I lay my head back on my couch. I have been so wrapped up in myself the last few days, I missed that Gemma needed me. She is always there for me and has been from the first day she walked into the salon. If she needs some girl time, that's what she will get.

I was serious about the bath and pull myself up from the couch. My body aches from more than just being on my feet all day. When I open the bedroom door and turn on the light, the sight of my bed reminds me of the other reason I am sore. Max and I had quite the night last night.

While the bath fills with hot water, I roam back to the kitchen and open a bottle of wine. It's a red that I haven't tried before. Wine is the one thing I spend a little money on. I like trying new and different bottles. I grab a glass out of the cabinet and pour. The first taste lets me know this one will be a keeper.

Once I'm back in the bathroom, I light the candles on the counter, turn off the water and the lights, then climb into the inviting tub. My bathroom may be small, but it is a place I love to relax. I lay back in the tub and close my eyes, thinking back to the text from Max. I still haven't answered it. I shouldn't ignore him, but I can't give in tonight. I can't have him come over for a third straight night. I need some time away from him.

With my mind made up, I grab my phone from the floor beside the tub and type out a quick message.

No plans. Calling it an early night after a long day at work.

Before I can drop the phone back to the floor, it dings. A glance shows it is from Max.

Want company? I'll bring dinner.

I do want company, his company. And I haven't eaten. *Don't give in, Tiba.* My mind tells me to stay strong.

I type: *I'm really tired. Somebody kept me up most of the night. Need some sleep.*

Part of me hopes he takes no for the answer and part of me hopes he decides to come anyway. I drop the phone on the floor and take a sip of wine. Before I can relax back in the tub, the phone dings again. I grab it up to see what he says, entirely too excited about these text messages.

What if I bring burgers and leave after we eat? Just visit for a little bit. I'll be good, I promise.

How can I say no to that? He is going to bring me food and just visit. No sex. I can do that. We have been friends for a long time, so this won't be anything more than that. Before I change my mind, I text back.

Okay. Burgers and chatting. No sex.

I get an almost immediate response.

No sex.

Even though I want to.

When the second message comes through, I can't help but laugh. I take a sip of wine and think about how to respond. Playful Max is so attractive. Does he need to know I want to just as much? Probably not. I decide to be vague but leave it open.

Not tonight, big guy. Someone is too sore to even think about it.

Imagining the expression on Max's face when he reads that message, I lean back in tub bringing my phone with me. I watch the dots on the screen as Max type and smile when a message appears.

Hmmm. I know something that would make that feel all better.

Oh no, buster. That leads to other things. NOT happening tonight.

My wine glass in one hand and my phone in the other, I watch the dots again. I have forgotten how much fun it can be to flirt with someone. A ding and a message. I smile from ear to ear.

Okay, okay. I'm going to get the food. I'll be good. See you soon.

I can't stop grinning at the screen. I drop the phone back over the side of the tub and finish my glass of wine. I shouldn't be playing with fire with Max and remind myself that heartbreak is coming. That's okay though because I'm going to have some great memories when it happens.

After I dry off and straighten the bathroom, I thumb through my closet for something to wear. Lounge pants and a big t-shirt are what I decide on. There is nothing sexy about the outfit, so Max shouldn't want to do more than chat. One last look in the mirror and I wander back into the kitchen for another glass of wine while I wait.

Chapter 11

MAX

WITH A SMILE ON MY face, I pull into the drive-thru at the burger joint. Tiba has no idea I had already ordered the food. When I went home after work, I planned to stay in and not think about her. That didn't work. It seems she is *all* I think about lately. So, I decided to order some food and show up at her apartment. Her text just happened to come when I was about to pull out of my driveway.

After I pay for the food, I turn my truck in the direction of her apartment. Tiba brings out a side of me I am not used to. I don't joke around with women. I take them out. I have sex with them. I don't play around with them—I especially don't text them back and forth.

Those thoughts make me realize that I feel something totally different for Tiba. Something I have never felt before. I don't want to try to put a name on it just yet, but I do want to enjoy it. Her insistence on not having a relationship concerns me a little because I really want to see where this is going to go with us, even though I initially told her it was one night only. I'll just have to wear her down on the relationship thing.

A thought hits me feels like a knife in my chest. What if she is seeing someone else? I never asked her once she cleared up that she wasn't on a date with Moss that night. What if there is another guy hanging in the wings? My hand rubs my chest in an effort to make the instant pain go away. Why does this woman make me feel like I am about to have a heart attack?

Pulling up to the gate of the apartment complex, I type in her apartment number to get her to buzz me in. Her surprised voice comes through the small speaker. "Hello?" Just the sound of her voice makes me feel better, but I still need to get this other guy stuff straight.

"Hey. It's me. Buzz me in."

"Okay." I hear a buzz almost at the same time as her response. The gate moves slowly as it opens. I am anxious, and it isn't moving fast enough for me. My fingers tap on the steering wheel while I wait. Now that I'm here, I'm ready to see Tiba. I am also ready to make sure there is no one else. As soon as there is room for my truck to make it through the gate, I hit the gas and barrel through. After parking quickly, I jog up the stairs to the apartment.

When I reach the landing at the top of the stairs, Tiba waits at the door to her apartment. She has on a t-shirt that swamps her small frame. Who knew a big t-shirt could be so sexy? The sight of her leaned against the door frame takes my breath away. It's going to be tough to stick to my promise of no sex tonight.

"You got here quick, big guy." Tiba gives me a smirk. "If I didn't know better, I would think you were already on your way over here."

I hold my hands up in admission, the bag of burgers hanging from one of them. "You caught me." I lean over and kiss her. It is supposed to be quick, but it's so good to feel her lips I let it drag on longer than intended. Her cheeks are flushed when I finally break away from her. "I had already ordered the burgers and was leaving my house when I got your message."

"Considering me as a sure thing, were you?" Tiba jokes as she waves me inside.

"Never. Just wanted to see you tonight. Before we go in, I have to ask you a question. You aren't seeing anyone else, are you?"

"No." One word that removes the knife that's been in my chest for the last few minutes.

Tiba grabs the bag from my hand and I follow her into the kitchen. She grabs a couple of paper plates out of the cabinet and unwraps the burgers.

"I just got one bag of fries. Thought we could share." I grab the fries out of the bag and start dividing them between the plates.

"Glass of wine?" Tiba asks and holds her glass for me to see.

"I'm more of a beer guy. Have any?"

She opens the refrigerator door and grabs a bottle of beer. She pops the top and passes it to me.

"Of course, I do. I love my wine, but there's nothing like a good beer." She picks up a plate and hands it to me.

This girl intrigues me more and more. I want to peel back the layers of her and learn all there is to know. For some reason, I don't think that will be an easy task. I follow her into the living room and sit beside her on the couch. I realize there is no dining table in her apartment. As I look around, I don't know where one would fit. She does have a coffee table that we use for our plates and drinks.

"You want to watch TV?" Tiba asks me.

"Nah. I'm not much of a TV watcher." I'm not much of a conversationalist either so this might be an interesting evening.

"Okay." Tiba takes a bite of her burger. "This burger is great. I don't eat a lot of meat, but when I do, it's soooo good." She groans as she takes another bite. The sound heads directly south on my body and does things I don't need to happen tonight.

Without touching my food, I continue to watch Tiba eat. Who knew eating could be so sexy? The little noises she makes with every bite are almost as good as the ones she makes when I am inside her. I'm hard as a rock and not the least bit interested in my food. Tiba notices that my gaze is on her.

"What?" she asks with her burger almost to her mouth. "Do I have something on my face?" She wipes around her mouth with the napkin.

"Nope." I shake my head and reach for her. With one hand behind her neck, I pull her in for a slow, soft kiss. "You are just awfully sexy when you eat."

She giggles and pushes my chest with one finger. "I think your mind is in the gutter. You need to get it out of there and eat."

With a chuckle, I settle back on the couch, safely away from her by a foot or two. Tiba's playful nature is one of the things I love about her. *Whoa, love?* Is that what these weird feelings have been. Surely not. Love can't happen in two days. I put that thought out of my mind and begin to eat. Tiba is right, this is one good burger.

We eat in a comfortable silence. It makes me happy to be able to enjoy quiet time with her. When we finish our meal, I grab our plates and napkins to toss them in the trash. I love when cleaning up means being able to throw away what you used. I refill Tiba's wine glass and grab myself another beer. She doesn't seem to mind that I make myself at home in her place.

After I drop back down beside Tiba and hand her the wine glass, I can't help myself and lean over to kiss her again. She responds and I feel her tongue gently wisp across my lips. It's all the invitation I need. I place my beer on the table without breaking our connection. With both hands now on her cheeks, I tilt her head slightly and allow myself to fully delve into the kiss. My promise of no sex tonight is getting harder and harder to keep. We are both breathless as I pull back.

"Can't keep that up and keep my promise." I caress Tiba's cheek before I move to the other end of the couch, seeking some separation between us. She smooths the ends of the big shirt she wears as if she is nervous, her nipples prominent against the thin material. After a moment, she raises her eyes to meet mine across the space.

"You stay over there, big guy. You *are* keeping that promise." She tucks her legs under her on the couch and lays her head against the back cushions. That's another thing I love about her, her ability to face something head on if she wants it. *Love.* There's that word again. Why? Why does it continue to pop up into my mind? Ready to move away from thoughts of love and even more ready to stop thinking about devouring Tiba, I decide to try to get to know her a little better.

"Fine, fine," I joke. "I'll stay over here, but you have to stay over there."

"Not a problem. I'm good right here."

"So, since we're not going to have sex, I guess we'll talk. I'm not a great talker but I'll give it a shot."

"I think you do just fine. What do you want to talk about?"

"I don't know. I don't usually spend a lot of time talking to women."

"Just jump into sex, huh, big guy." Tiba pulls one of her legs from underneath her and kicks her foot against my leg.

"Something like that. I've never wanted to talk to them though. They never meant anything to me." Suddenly I am embarrassed about my past. I've never thought about it until now. I have been an ass when it comes to women.

"Because you love Gemma, right?" Tiba looks away as she asks the question. It's time I clear this up. Her foot still rests against my leg, so I lift it with my hand and begin to massage it.

"Hey, look at me." Tiba brings her gaze back to mine. I see sadness in her eyes, something I never want to see when she is with me. "The answer to that is yes and no. Yes, I thought I loved Gemma, so yes, I used those women. But no, I am *not* in love with Gemma." Tiba tilts her head to the side as she tries to understand my words.

"Just a few days ago you were in love with her? How are you suddenly not?"

"Mom has told me for a while that I wasn't in

love with Gemma. That the love I feel was friendly, not *in love*." I pause. How do I explain this where Tiba will understand without baring my soul about what she has made me feel? Or should I just tell her? I decide to tell her. There's no reason to hide from her. "It seems there is a tiny, crazy-haired woman that burst into my life and made me realize my Mom is the smartest woman in the world."

There, I said it. Now the ball is in Tiba's court. I hold my breath in anticipation of her response. She watches me as she processes what I have said. I begin to wonder if she is ever going to speak when she finally breaks the silence.

"So, you *aren't* in love with Gemma?"

"That's what I am saying."

"And you think I'm the reason?"

"I didn't say that. You are the reason I *realized* I'm not in love with her. There's a difference. I had let myself obsess over her for years *thinking* I was in love."

"And how did I change that?" Tiba continues to watch me. Why is she asking so many questions?

"After being with you, it seems that you are the only woman I think about. I feel things with you I haven't felt with anyone else. I don't want to label it, but I know without a doubt that I never felt this way about Gemma." There's no way to say it any clearer since I don't fully understand it myself.

"Max," Tiba says my name as she pulls her foot from my hand, "I don't know what to think about this. I mean, you were married to Gemma and she's my best friend. Now, after we jumped into bed together, you say you never loved her. Heck, just a few weeks ago, you tried to stop her from marrying Raef." And there it is. My stupidity comes back to haunt me yet again. I slide across the couch to be closer to Tiba.

"Look. I don't have a clue what this thing is between us." I point my finger back and forth between the two of us. "What I do know is that *this* isn't anything Gemma and I had. You know our history. We'd been best buds for years and when her parents died, I thought if I married her, it would be the right thing. Yes, at the time, I thought I loved her. I was young and wanted to take care of her. Now, I know that wasn't the right move. Gemma will always be one of my closest friends, but I *am not* in love with her. And if you want to get down to it, you showed me that. *This* . . . " I point between us again, "*this* is why I know Mom was right. *This* is worth exploring."

I take Tiba's hand in mine because she looks like she might bolt from the couch. She won't look me directly in the eye, which is odd for her. I try to decipher what I see in her expression, but it is a mixture of so many things. On top of confusion, it almost looks like fear.

"Hey, look at me," I tell her softly. She slowly brings her gaze back to mine. After only a moment, she tries to pull her eyes away again. I gently touch her cheek and turn her back to me.

"I don't do relationships, Max," she whispers.

"I know. And I don't either . . . until now." I kiss her forehead and pull her onto my lap. "What do you say we don't give it a name? Let's just enjoy it."

Tiba is stunning with her head on my chest, tilted upward where I can see her face. She is at war with her emotions and it shows on that gorgeous face. I hate to see her so conflicted. My lips brush hers in the softest of kisses.

"I don't know . . . "

I kiss her again because that isn't the answer I want to hear. I don't push the kiss, just keep it gentle.

Finally, she pulls back and says, "No name, no relationship. We'll just enjoy."

Yes! My inner self does a fist pump. It's not where I want to be, but it is a step in the right direction. Time to back off some and just get to know each other.

"Enough of the deep talk. How about mindless conversation?" Tiba relaxes in my arms. "We've known each other for years, but we don't really *know* each other. I now know you like beer even though you're a wine girl. You know I don't like TV. How about truck or car?"

Tiba laughs against my chest. "Such a guy question. Car of course." The sound of her laughter makes me smile.

"Hey, now. Trucks are the best."

"Cold weather or warm weather?" Tiba asks as she leans back against the pillow at the end of the couch. She is stretched across my lap where I can see all of her.

"I guess warm since we live in Louisiana and I spend most of my time working outside. You?"

"Cold. I've always wanted to go where there is snow. This heat here is a killer." Her expression is wistful. I tuck this tidbit of information in my memory. Maybe one day I can take her to see real snow.

"Here's a good one. Burgers or pizza? I'm a

burger guy, hence the ones tonight." Tiba rewards me with a smirk.

"Mr. Meat Eater, huh? Pizza for me, but I do love a good burger."

"Can't help it, I like my meat."

"So do I, big guy, so do I." She gives me a wicked grin to make sure I understand what she means. I know exactly what she means, and it hits me directly in the groin. I grab her and press her against my now very present erection. She giggles as she wiggles away from it.

"Can't talk like that, woman. No sex tonight, remember."

Tiba laughs as she takes her hand and rubs against my erection. "Poor Max. Do you think you will survive?"

"Keep that up and I might not." I pull her hand away from me. I love the way she teases me, but I am determined to keep my promise to her. She gives me a pout, but I can see she has to fight to back a smile. In one swift move, I maneuver us on the couch where we are now lying facing each other, her wrapped in my arms.

Tiba sighs in contentment, and I smile at the sound. My chin rests on the top of her head, her curls tickling my neck. Who knew I would enjoy such light-hearted conversation and cuddling on a couch? Hell, I've never *cuddled* before this woman. I thought I was too much of a manly man for that. Plus, I never wanted to hang around long enough for that either.

"Flowers or candy?" I ask. I've never sent either, but suddenly want to know her preference.

"Flowers." Tiba's voice is softer now. "They represent the beauty in the world. Country or city?"

"That one's easy. Country all the way. What about you? You seem like the city kind."

"Country. I've had my fill of the city. Won't go back." Tiba sighs but this time it doesn't sound like a happy one. I want to press for more on the subject but this isn't the time. Pulling her a little tighter to me, I kiss the top of her head. She relaxes against me again.

We continue our little game until Tiba's words are so quiet I can barely hear them. I stop the questions and in only a few minutes, her breaths even out and she is asleep against me. Grabbing the blanket off the back of the couch, I cover us both with it, making sure not to wake her in the process. I shift us a little to get in a more comfortable position.

After tonight, I am even more confused about what this is between us. Tiba brings out a side of me I didn't even know I had. In the matter of a few days, I have gone from a brusque guy who didn't care about much to someone who spent the night enjoying nothing but chatting while holding this beautiful woman.

As I drift off to sleep, my mind brings up that one word again, *love*.

Chapter 12

TIBA

THE BELL ON THE FRONT door of the salon dings as it opens. A quick look at the clock tells me it's not time for my next appointment. She must have come a little early. I quickly close my lunch and toss it in the fridge before I walk to the front of the shop. Instead of my next client, there is a delivery man with a huge arrangement of flowers. He must be in the wrong place.

"Can I help you?" I ask politely.

"I have a delivery for Tiba Ramon." The guy reads from the card that hangs from the flowers.

"Um, I'm Tiba." I step a little closer to him, curious at this point. He doesn't say anything else and extends the vase in my general direction. Before he can drop it, I grab it and hold it closer to me. As soon as I have it in my grasp, he scuttles out the door.

Standing frozen in the middle of the salon, I hold the most beautiful peach roses I have ever seen. A quick count tells me there are a dozen of them surrounded by baby's breath and greenery. After a few moments of gazing at them, I finally move to place them on my station.

A white envelope with my name hangs from the front of the bouquet. The suspense overwhelms me, but I can't seem to get my fingers to reach for it. Who would send me flowers? What if it's *him?* What if he's found me? I know he's still in prison, but he has always had his ways. The fear overwhelms me. Do I want to know? Knowing I have to see where they came from, I grab the card and unpin it from the bow. My hands shake as I pull the card out of its little envelope. I can barely focus my eyes on the writing.

It's not snow, but I hope you like the flowers. Thanks for last night.   Max

I fall back into the chair at my station. Max sent me flowers. Max Greenwood sent me flowers. All the fear dissipates with the happiness that flows through me. My past hasn't found me, *and* Max sent me flowers. Tossing my head back, I giggle and spin the chair around in circles.

When I stop spinning, I am dizzy but happy. I have loved Max for so long and no one knew. It's still that way, but now. . . now, I share something with him. Something that has no name but is real. Oh, how I wish I could see it through. The thought threatens the glee in my heart, but I tramp it back down. I'm going to enjoy whatever time I have with Max. The front door jingles again and I tear my gaze from my gift to see my client.

The next hours are spent in pleasant comradery with my customers. We laugh and joke while I work. I catch up on their lives, a part of my job I really enjoy. Just as I finish the last head of hair, the front door flies open as Gemma bursts through.

"Something chasing you, girlie?" I chuckle at the

grimace on her face.

"No, silly. It's just hot out there." Gemma takes her long hair in her hands and pulls it up off her neck. The flowers catch her attention and her head pops my direction with curiosity bright in her eyes. "Flowers?"

"Um, yea. Flowers." I grab the broom to sweep up the hair from the floor. "You're a little early. I still need to clean up the shop."

"Raef talked me into taking Charley to Alexis until he gets home from work. Don't change the subject. Where'd the flowers come from?"

Gemma moves to pick up the card that sits next to the vase. I drop the broom and try to grab the card from her, but she has already read it. She stares at the card for what seems like an eternity before she raises her gaze to meet mine.

"Max sent you flowers?" Gemma's head tilts to the side. The lines across her forehead tell me how confused she is. There is no way I can hide this from her any longer. I have to tell her the truth, she is my best friend. I drop into the chair at the station Gemma previously used and point to the chair at mine. She sits, the card still in her hand.

"Where do I start?" I say without thinking.

"The beginning would be a good place." Gemma sounds hurt.

"Gem, don't be upset that I didn't tell you. This just happened a few days ago."

"Were you going to tell me?"

"I don't know," I admit. "He's your ex-husband. And you know that this can't go anywhere with him. You know my past."

"Tiba!" Gemma exclaims. "You know my past,

too. You know there's nothing between Max and me. I would never stop the two of you from being together."

"You say that, but he told you he loved you right before your wedding. He is your past and you're my best friend. I'm not sure what to do with that."

"I honestly don't have a problem with the two of you being together. In fact, I think it would be great! You know my feelings for Max are purely platonic. He's like a brother to me and will always be one of my best friends, but he'll never be more than that. As far as what Max feels for me, I don't know what to tell you. I really don't think he loves me like he claims to. But you'd have to work that out with him. I definitely don't want to see him hurt you."

"He says he realizes that he doesn't have those type of feelings for you, you know, *real* love." Recognizing what I just said, I search Gemma's expression. "I'm sorry, I didn't mean to say it that way. I hope I didn't hurt your feelings."

"If anything, that makes me very happy, not hurt. I don't want him to feel that way for me. You know that, Raef knows that, and most of all, Max knows that."

"Oh, Gem. I don't know what's happening." I sink further down into the chair.

"Start from the beginning and let's work through it."

For the next several minutes, I tell Gemma about the last few nights with Max. She breaks out in a huge smile as soon as I start talking and doesn't stop all the way through. Once I finish with every-thing up to the flowers that were delivered today, she practically bounces in the chair.

"What has you so dang happy over there?" I ask her, exhausted from baring my soul to her.

"You. Max. You and Max together!" She jumps from the chair and grabs me into a hug. Gemma is a hugger. "This is great! The two people I love the most after my husband and child are together! And obviously happy." She breaks into a silly dance.

"Calm down over there. This thing with Max is great, but it isn't going anywhere."

She stops in front of me. "Why not?"

"Gemma. Be real. You know my situation. You know all the reasons I can't have a long-term relationship with anyone." My eyes drop to the floor. Gemma is the only person that knows I am married. The only one who knows my husband almost killed me and is prison. The only friend I have who knows he will never let me have anyone else, even though he is behind bars and has no clue where I am.

Gemma has dropped to the floor in front of me, her hands on my knees. She stares at me with determination.

"We will fix this. Daniel, Raef's brother, is an attorney. We. Can. Fix. This."

"I don't know, Gem. If I try to force the divorce, *he* may find out where I am. If he finds that out, he'll send someone. You know that. I don't want to have to run, I like it here. And I don't want Max in the middle of something like that." The fear of my husband is real. He has said he will never let me go. He will send his brother's goons for me if he finds me. With his gang connections, it wouldn't be hard to make me disappear or to harm Max.

"Tiba, listen to me. Before, we didn't have the money to make sure he didn't find you. We didn't have connections." Gemma stands and waves her hands in the air. "My husband has the money and the connections. Let us help you. Raef will help you."

"I'm scared." There. I said it. The words at the heart of everything.

"I know." Gem plops back in the chair across from me. She leans forward, elbows propped on her knees. "Tell me one thing. Do you love Max?"

The question causes me to jerk my head up, my eyes larger than normal. I'm pretty sure I look like a deer caught in headlights. "What?" I squeak, unable to find my voice.

"Do you love Max?" She repeats the question. I feel the wetness of tears as they slide down my cheeks. Nodding, I drop my head into my hands. Gemma is in front of me again and takes my hands away from my face. She wipes the tears away. "You have for a while, haven't you?"

"How'd you know?"

"I've suspected for a while. Remember, I know you better than anyone else." Gemma grins from ear to ear. I break into a grin of my own.

"I guess I am an open book to you. I just thought I did a better job of hiding it." I shake my head and my frown returns, etched into my skin. "But it doesn't matter. I can't bring Max into the middle of my screwed-up past. I could never give him the life he deserves."

"Come on." Gemma grabs pulls me out of the chair. "Let's get this place cleaned up and get some pizza. We'll celebrate you guys tonight. Tomorrow we'll start the path to solve your problem."

Gemma tosses the towels in the washer while I grab the broom to finish sweeping. Once the shop is clean, we grab our purses and head out. We walk the short distance to the pizza place and chat mindlessly on the way. It's such a relief that Gemma knows about Max. I find myself almost believing that she and Raef can help me, that Max and I actually have a chance.

Chapter 13

MAX

AS I HANG UP THE phone, I lean back in the desk chair. For a day that started out perfectly it went to hell and back quickly. Now I am completely exhausted. My eyes close before I hear a knock on the door to the job site office. Before I can say anything, Jerry walks in. I sit up straighter as he flops into the chair across the desk from me.

"We've got it all cleaned up out there." Jerry looks as tired as I feel.

"Good. Sorry I've been stuck in here all day. I'm sick of the phone, but I have security lined up for after hours."

The cost of the security will eat into the company's profits significantly, but we can't have another incident like last night. We arrived this morning to an open gate and a vandalized work site. Even part of the structure we are building was damaged. After the police swept the scene, the day was spent cleaning up. A day of construction lost.

"Tha' cops got any idea who did it?" Jerry questions.

"Nope. None at all." I fidget with the pencil on top of the desk. I pushed for this job against my father's advice. It falling apart now is not an option.

"Ya' think it has to do with them threats ya' got before?" Jerry refers to when we were first awarded the job and I received a letter along with some anonymous phone calls. The threats were to try to scare me off and I didn't take them too seriously at the time. Nothing happened from them, so I thought they had backed off when they realized we were going to stick with the job. Now, I wonder.

"I honestly don't know, Jerry. Looks like it might be connected. Question is, who?"

"Bound to be one of tha' big men from tha' city. Those guys play dirty. Your pop warned ya' about 'em." Jerry's jaw ticks with the anger that resides beneath the surface of his words. He values this company as much as my father and I do.

"Saying I told you so?" The words come out with a bite. "I know, Jerry. I put us in this position by taking this job. But, if we can hang in there and finish it, we will be on the same playing field as those big guys from the city." I throw my arm in the direction of New Orleans. Frustration bubbles from me as I reach my boiling point for the day.

"Not sayin' nothin' like that. Jus' sayin' we gotta be careful. This may jus' be tha' beginnin'."

"So, how do we prove who's behind this? I've got security lined up, but no way to tie this mess to anyone." I slam the pencil on the desktop. "The worst part of the whole day was having to call Dad and tell him what happened."

"Hmmm."

"Yeah, that's about what I thought too. I could hear the disappointment in his voice."

"Hmmm."

"God, Jerry. Can't you say something?" I yell.

"Nothin' to say, boy. Ya' wanted tha' job. Ya' jus' gotta' hang with it."

Not able to sit still any longer, I jump out of my chair and pace back and forth in the tiny office space. Both hands run through my hair as my anger builds. Who did this? And why?

"Calm down, son," Jerry says as he stands and grabs me by the shoulder. "It's all gonna' be okay. This day's over. Go home an' get some rest. Morrow's anotha' day."

"I will. As soon as the security guard gets here." As soon as the words come out of my mouth, there's a knock on the door. "That must be him now." I grab the door and swing it open. Sure enough, there's a huge man in a uniform standing before me. I'm a big guy but this man dwarfs me.

We make quick introductions and Jerry leaves to go home. I show the guard around the construction site so he has a feel of the place. Before I head out for the night, I make sure he has my number in his phone and knows to call me if anything looks out of the ordinary. Tomorrow his company will be here to put up surveillance cameras but tonight, the only eyes I have here will be his.

Once I'm satisfied that the security guy has everything under control, I lock the gate with him inside. I still can't believe it has come to this. Frustration and anger courses through my body. My nerve endings feel like they are on fire, almost like I could jump out of my skin. For the first time in my life, I want to talk to someone about my day. That someone would be Tiba. I grab my phone out of my pocket and shoot off a text as soon as I sit down in my truck.

Hey. Can I see you tonight?

When I don't get an immediate response, I put the truck in drive and ease out of the parking lot. A part of me wants to stay the night here, but I have to put my faith in the company I hired to watch over things. As soon as I pull into the road, my phone dings with a message. I see it's from Tiba and open it as soon as I pull up to the stop sign at the end of the road.

Later. Dinner with Gem.

Tiba told me this morning that she was going out with Gemma tonight, but I had forgotten. She said they needed some girl time. After a glance in the rear-view mirror to make sure I'm not holding anyone up, I message her back.

Later is good. My place tonight. Come over whenever you want.

With the day I've had, I want to take a hot shower and relax instead of getting back out to go to her place. Of course, if she wants me to go over there, I will definitely do it. I suddenly remember that Tiba has never been to my house, so I quickly text her the address before she has time to respond. My phone dings and a quick look shows me she has agreed.

When I pull into my garage, I let out a sigh of relief. My home is my sanctuary, my one happy place. Dad and I built the entire house ourselves, only farming out the plumbing and electrical work. My blood, sweat, and yes, tears, are in this house. I made it exactly the way I wanted it and didn't rush any part of it. It took two years to complete, but it was worth it.

I throw my keys on the kitchen counter when I get inside. My priority is to grab a beer out of the fridge. I pop the top off the bottle and turn it up for a large swig. My gaze wanders around the open living area of my home. The pride I feel in the place that usually calms me does nothing tonight. Instead, I'm reminded that I made a choice with the family business that may bring it down. My grip tightens on the beer bottle and I down the remainder of the liquid.

Knowing Tiba is coming over, I spend a little time straightening up the house. I don't keep a messy place, but I am a typical guy and don't always pick up behind myself like I should. After I throw the dishes in the dishwasher and make sure there are no random clothing items dropped anywhere, I head to my bathroom.

A shower helps my mood a little. It could be the body jets that worked on the tense muscles in my back. Whatever the case, I'm glad to feel a little better. I wrap a towel around my waist and trek back to the kitchen. Just as I get another beer out of the fridge, the doorbell rings. Tiba must be here. I grab a second beer and greet her with it at the door.

"Wow, big guy." She takes the bottle as she walks through the door. Her eyes roam my towel-clad body as she passes. "That's a pretty nice welcome."

"Glad to please." I laugh. "Sorry about the beer. I don't have any wine here."

"Not a problem. Remember, I'm a beer girl too."

Tiba's gaze wanders around my home. Her eyes widen in shock as she sees the living area. I can't help but smile as she takes in the huge stone fire-place and oversized leather furniture. She stops when she sees the matching lamps on the tables and the framed photos that sit below them. She picks up a picture of Charley and then one of my parents. She wasn't expecting what she sees. When she looks back to me, her mouth is agape.

"Like it?" I ask.

"I love it! I figured you had a typical bachelor pad, but this—this is amazing." Tiba's arms wave around the room in wonder.

"Thanks. I'm pretty proud of it. Dad and I built every inch of this place. Took a couple of years, but it turned out just like I wanted." I take a drink of the beer and chuckle. "Now the decorating part. I paid someone to do that. I'm not much into the matching throw pillows and stuff."

"That makes more sense. I wondered if you had *that* much style." Her laughter tinkles in the room.

"Look around all you want. There are two bed-rooms and an office that way, kitchen is over there." I point each direction, then tilt my head toward the master bedroom. "I'm going to put on some clothes."

Tiba nods and moves in the directions of the other bedrooms. As she walks away from me, I have a vision of her becoming part of this home. I shake the thought out of my head. I'm getting way ahead of myself. In my room, I grab a pair of basketball shorts and t-shirt. Now's not the time to push. It's time to enjoy the night and turn a horrible day around.

Chapter 14

TIBA

WHEN MAX OPENED THE DOOR, the last
thing I expected to see was his rock-hard
body in nothing but a towel. I couldn't help my
eyes travelling from head to toe over his body. His
wet hair created a stunning sight against his golden
skin. The towel hung low on his hips, tempting me
to grab it. His paler legs show he works outside in
the sun regularly. Obviously, he works without a
shirt most of the time because that chest is like a
tan Adonis. I have never seen a man more gorgeous
than Max Greenwood.

Once inside his home, I am astonished at the
interior. He doesn't live the typical single man's
house. His furniture is masculine but not overly
so. His walls are adorned with pictures of various types of boats, an interest I recently learned
he shares with his father. The focal point of the
room is a massive television on the wall above a
rock surrounded fireplace. Everything is simple
but tasteful. After learning he hired a decorator, it
all makes more sense. When Max offers for me to
explore the rest of his house, I jump at the chance.
I grab one more glance at his glorious body before

I wander toward the area he said was more bed-
rooms and an office.

The first room I find is a bedroom. I am shocked
at the size of it. I think this room is bigger than my
apartment and it's only a guest room. I wander in
and run my hand along the bed rail. It must be at
least a queen-sized bed. The room is full of furniture, and still has tons of floor space. I notice an
attached bathroom and venture to check it out. It's
large and as beautiful as the rest of the house. The
bathroom leads to the second bedroom in a Jack-
and-Jill style. This room is identical to the other
one in size. Each bedroom is decorated in a different theme. One is blue with a nautical theme,
while the other is green with an outdoors theme.

When I venture back into the hall, I cross to what
must be the office. The first thing I notice is this
room is a little messier than the rest of the house,
showing me that Max actually uses this room. A
huge desk covered with papers centers the room.
There is a laptop and another massive computer
screen on an extension from the desk. As I look
at the walls, a sound catches my attention. I turn
to see Max leaned against the door frame as he
watches me.

"My office stays a mess." Max pushes off the door
and walks behind me, wrapping his arms around
my waist. My body heats immediately from the
feel of him against me. "I spend a lot of time in
here at night. Especially at the beginning of a new
project."

"These photos?" I gesture to the framed pictures
on the wall of various houses and other buildings.

"All jobs our company has done. I started this on

the first project my dad let me have a real role in. I had always helped him here and there as a kid, but this one. . ." Max releases me and walks down the room to point at a photo of a house. "This one was the first one where I was a real paid employee. I was sixteen. When we finished the house, I was exhausted but so proud to have been a part of creating something so grand for someone. I took the picture to remember that feeling. It kind of became a tradition after that." He glances down the wall at the other photos. The pride he feels in his work emanates from his body. This simple house tour has shown me so much of what makes up Max Greenwood. I've learned more about him in his home than he could have ever told me with words. From the family photos and the outdoor themed décor, to this wall in his office, it's like a view inside Max's head.

"I like the tradition. You may need to build a bigger office one day though." One wall is already almost full. He smiles and pulls me back against him.

"I still have the other walls." He kisses me gently after he turns me to face him. "But from now on, I know just who I want to take the pictures of my completed jobs."

"Who's that?" I ask as I stand on my toes to kiss Max again. He eagerly responds to my kiss. When we finally break apart, he responds.

"You."

"Me? Why me?"

"I've seen your photos. You're amazing behind a camera. You've just become the photographer for Greenwood Construction."

"Oh, wow. Okay. As long as they are just for in here."

"We'll see." He grabs my hand. "Have you eaten? I'm starving." Just like that he changes the subject. I'll make sure to bring it up again when the time comes.

"Gemma and I had pizza earlier, but I could probably eat a little something."

Max doesn't let go of my hand until we reach the kitchen. He opens the refrigerator to explore the contents. After he pushes things around for a few minutes, he looks over the top of the door.

"I'm not much of a cook. I can make a mean sandwich though." His sheepish grin is almost boyish. Smiling, I push him aside to see exactly what he has in there.

"Stand back, big guy. I'm a pretty good cook. I'm sure I can make something with what you have in here." It's obvious he doesn't cook much based on the food he has. After a brief search, I come out with a pack of hamburger meat, cheese and an onion. "Do you have any noodles?" Max laughs and points to a cabinet. I have better luck there as I find not only noodles, but canned tomatoes and a row of spices.

"Mom stocks the cabinet when she's in town. I never use much out of it." He shrugs his shoulders and that grin adorns his face again.

"Spoiled much?" I raise my eyebrow at him.

"Maybe a little."

Max grabs us each another beer and I start to put together a meal. I rummage through the cabinets and find a large pot. As I fill it with water, he plops down on the other side of the large kitchen island.

He watches me while I put the noodles on to cook and begin to cut the onion.

"I can't do much with what you have, but we should have a good pot of spaghetti soon." I glance up from the knife to find his eyes glued to me. I give him a smile and resume my work.

Max and I chat while I cook. While I create an amazing sauce with the tomatoes and spices, I tell him about my evening with Gemma. He is thrilled to know that we are no longer a secret and I admit that it's a weight off of me too. I worry about keeping my past a secret from him, but if Gemma is right and Daniel can help me, I won't have to for much longer.

When the spaghetti is almost ready, I throw together what I call poor man's garlic bread. All it takes is regular sliced bread, butter and a little garlic seasoning. Fortunately, Max has those things and before we know it, everything is ready.

He grabs plates from the cabinet and we fill them quickly. We choose to sit at the counter of the island instead of the table in the dining area. It's a nice, cozy atmosphere and I'm shocked at how comfortable I feel here. It almost feels like home. I stop myself from continuing that thought. Max and I are a long way from anything like that.

He tears into his meal like a man starved. I chuckle as I watch before tasting it myself. I am my biggest critic when it comes to my cooking, but this turned out pretty good considering what I had to work with. Max quickly puts away almost half of his plate of food.

"Wow, Tiba! This is great! Where'd you learn to cook like this?" he asks as he shovels another mouthful.

"My mother is Italian. I've been cooking as long as I can remember."

"I can tell. Italian. Is your dad Italian too?" Max asks as I realize I have just spilled a part of my life I never discuss. My parents are no longer a part of my life and never will be. Why did I just tell him about my mother? I find myself wanting to tell him more which is totally out of character for me.

"No. My father's not Italian, he's black. He says he's of Creole descent. You should have been able to figure out from my skin and hair that I'm mixed."

"I never really knew. Now that I know, I can see features of both ethnicities in you. To me, you're just a beautiful woman. So, have you been to Italy?"

"No. My mother met my father in New Orleans on a family trip. They fell in love immediately, much to the dismay of her parents. When it was time to go back to Italy, she wouldn't go. Her parents disowned her on the spot. They wanted no part of their daughter with a black man." I pause and take a drink from my beer. It's still hard for me to understand how they could be so intolerant of my parents' relationship. Of course, I know times were different back then, but to leave their daughter on a completely different continent still blows me away. "She loved my father enough to let them leave."

"Wow. What a love story. So, you don't know any of your mom's people?"

"When I was a teenager, I wrote my grandmother without my mother's knowledge. I was shocked when she responded. After my mother found out, she tried to make me stop communicating with

Nonna, but I refused. Turns out my grandmother never wanted to cut my mother out of their lives, but she obeyed the wishes of my grandfather. He had since passed on, but she didn't know how to find her daughter. My letter connected us, and we wrote and talked on the phone until she died a few years ago." A tear forms in the corner of my eye and I quickly wipe it away. Nonna was the one person who didn't turn her back on me. I may never have met her in person, but I feel her loss every day. She knew me better than anyone in my life, even Gemma.

"Did your mom ever come around and talk to her?" Max seems genuinely interested and I can't seem to stop obliging him with information that I never share.

"No. To my mother, her parents died the day they got on the plane back to Italy. My father's family became her only family."

"That's sad. I guess there are always two sides to everything though." Max picks up his plate and takes it to the sink. I've lost my appetite with the conversation but continue to push the food around on my plate.

"I may be overstepping but do you ever see your parents?"

My gaze jumps from my plate with Max's question. He has no idea what a loaded question that is. A question I can't give him details when I answer. I stare into his eyes for a moment before I respond with a simple but forceful, "No."

He seems to get the message that this is an off-limits subject and doesn't pursue it. Needing to change the course of this conversation, I steer us away.

"So, let's change the topic. How was your day today?"

Max sighs and leans across the counter toward me.

"Today sucked."

I tilt my head to the side and the corner of my mouth drops into the sad expression I try to avoid.

"That is, until you got here . . . " he continues as he reaches across and takes one of my hands into his. His smile is contagious, and I find myself smiling as brightly back to him.

"What happened to make it suck?"

"When we got to the job this morning, someone had vandalized it overnight. Everything was scattered around the site and some of the work we had already completed had to be torn out and redone." My mouth drops open in shock and Max notices. "It's okay. We got everything fixed back to the state it was in before. It just meant a wasted day and I don't like to waste time like that."

"Who did it?" I ask so quietly it's almost a whisper.

"No clue. But if they show back up, I have security there now. Shouldn't happen again. We had some threats when we got the job because we were small and some of the larger companies felt assured they would win the bid. Then again, it could just be kids. Who knows?" Max settles back on the stool next to me.

Fear overtakes me. Could this be the work of my ex-husband's brother? Has Gerald found out from prison that I've spent time with Max? Could he have found me? I'm on the verge of hyperventilating. I can't bring this type of destruction down on Max.

I rise from my seat so fast I knock it over. The sound makes me jump in surprise and adds to the shakes that are already prominent enough on my body. Max picks up the chair and looks at me with a frown.

"Are you okay? I didn't mean to upset you with my day. We have it all worked out. No need to worry." Max's hands are on my arms. His frown is a mixture of concern and confusion. I move away from him and his arms drop to his sides.

"I . . . I have to go," I stutter. "I have to go now." I grab my purse from the table and rush to the door.

"Tiba. Wait! Don't go," Max calls after me.

I run out the door with Max on my heels. Without looking back, I hear him continue to call my name. Once ensconced in my car, I finally look at him. He stands on his porch with his arms in the air, silently asking, *What just happened here?* I drop my gaze and focus on backing my car out of his driveway. Only when I am driving away do I take one more glance in the rear-view mirror. Max stands in the same spot, frozen like a statue. Like a beautiful golden statue. Tears break free from my eyes and flow down my cheeks. My time with this man is over. Deep inside, I knew it would come. I fooled myself into thinking I could have a relationship.

When I make it to the main road, I stop and dial Gemma's number. The phone rings a few times before she picks up. I don't give her time to say hello before I speak.

"I think he's found me."

Chapter 15

MAX

I PULL UP TO THE JOB site at five in the morning. After a night of no sleep, I couldn't stay in the house any longer. I still have no idea what happened last night. Everything was fine until I told Tiba about what happened here at the job yesterday. After that, she just ran out. I don't have any clue as to why something here at my job would affect her that way. It's all so crazy. I've never seen her act like that before. She was shaking like she was afraid of something. Why would my job site being vandalized make her scared? Maybe she thinks being involved with me will lead to something bad happening to her. None of it makes any sense.

The guard meets me at the gate, shocked to see me so early. We chat for a few minutes and I send him on his way. I'm glad to hear he had no trouble overnight. The next hour is spent in the office, looking at plans and preparing for the day ahead. When the crew arrives, we all get to work. Being able to get out there today and swing a hammer relieves some of my stress.

By noon, that relief is gone when the security company arrives to install cameras on the site. I spend the rest of the afternoon with the installers as they place cameras in places I feel are strategic to capture anyone that might consider vandalizing our project again. I text Tiba repeatedly throughout the afternoon, but to no avail.

Once we finish with the camera install, the work day is just about over. I roam the site and check on everyone to make sure we are back on schedule. Jerry picks up on my mood and tries to talk but I shut him down quickly. I'm not in the mood to discuss what has me festered today, at least not with him. Since Tiba is avoiding me, the only person I want to talk to right now is Gemma. Maybe she can shed some light on what happened last night.

Since we have security cameras now, we won't have a guard on site at night. The company will have one of their mobile guards drive by and do a walk-through periodically each night until we finish the job. Making sure the gate is locked up tightly, I head to my truck. I pull the phone back out of my pocket and check my messages. Still nothing from Tiba.

When I pull out of the parking lot, I turn toward the salon. If she won't answer me, I will just go to her. Then again, I have no idea if she had late clients today or not. After the short drive, I find the salon locked. I guess that answers my question. I drive on to Tiba's apartment complex, stop at the gate, and put in her apartment number. No response. I punch it in again. Still no response. Either she is not there, or she is ignoring me. Neither option makes me happy. Even more frustrated than before, I grab my phone and dial Gemma's number.

"Hey, Max," Gemma answers.

"I need to talk to you. Can I run by the house?" I don't waste time with chit-chat. I need to speak to Gemma and I want to do it in person. She can't hide anything from me in person. That girl's expressions give everything away.

"Yes. Come on. We'll see you in few minutes." Gemma disconnects the call. She must know what happened. She never ends a call like that. She better be ready to tell me the truth.

My thoughts are of Tiba during the drive to Raef and Gemma's house. When she left my house last night, it felt final. It felt like a knife piercing my heart. Somewhere along the way, I have fallen head over heels for this sprite of a woman. Me. Max Greenwood. The man who swore he was in love with Gemma for so many years. I never felt this way about Gemma. What I feel for Tiba is so much more complex and deep. And now, so much more painful. I just *thought* my heart broke when Raef came back into Gemma's life. That was nothing compared to how I felt when Tiba left last night. Watching her drive away was the most painful thing I have experienced.

I pull down the long driveway of the Alvero home. While I park, I notice Charley bouncing on the porch. She waits until I kill the engine before she runs toward my truck. She's there before I can get out the door.

"Uncle Max! I'm so glad you're here!" Charley's little voice carries as she jumps in front of me with her hands in the air. I scoop her up into my arms and start toward the house with her.

"Hello there, Munchkin. I'm glad to see you too." I give Charley a kiss on the cheek while enjoying her tiny arms wrapped around my neck. This little one has had a piece of my heart since the day she was born.

Charley rambles on about her week as we walk into the house. I don't have to do much to respond other than the occasional nod. This child can talk non-stop. I spot Raef and Gemma in the kitchen once we get inside. I put Charley down when we reach the others and she finally takes a break in her chatter, giving me the opportunity to say the first thing that comes to my mind.

"Where the hell is she?" I throw it out there. No point in beating around the bush.

"Max!" Gemma exclaims.

"Where the hell is who, Uncle Max?" Charley spits out before anyone can say anything else. I realize why Gemma was upset now. I didn't even think about my language. I hear a subdued chuckle and look over to see Raef doing his best to contain his laughter.

"Charley!" Gemma's face is red with frustration.

"Dammit, I'm sorry." I realize I did it again. "I mean, I'm sorry."

"Max! What is wrong with you?" Gemma throws her hands in the air before she turns to Charley. "Charley, you know you aren't supposed to repeat bad words."

I shift on both feet in embarrassment. I didn't mean to get Charley in trouble. Usually I am much better about holding my tongue in front of her. Tiba has me all kinds of messed up right now.

"Come on, Charlotte." Raef grabs Charley by the hand, still doing his best to keep from exacerbating the situation. "Let's go clean up your playroom before we eat."

"I think that's a great idea." Gemma's lips are still pressed tightly together. She watches as Raef leads Charley from the room before she turns back to me. Her eyes flare bright with anger when they find mine. I duck my head in shame, knowing I have disappointed Gemma with Charley. "You've got to watch your mouth in the presence of my daughter, Max. She's like a sponge and will repeat whatever you say, even if she knows better. You know this!"

"I'm sorry, Gemma. I really am." I run both hands through my hair in my own frustration. "I just can't find Tiba and it has me on edge. She ran out on me last night for no reason and now she's disappeared." Dammit if I don't feel what may be a tear in my eye.

"I know." Gemma's voice is soft now. My head pops up with her words. Now she is the one whose eyes avoid mine.

"You know?"

"Yes, she came to me when she left last night."

"Is she okay? Why did she run out? Where is she?" I fire the questions one after another.

"She's okay. And she's out of town for a bit."

"Out of town? Where? Where is she, Gemma?"

"I can't tell you, Max. She needs to be alone."

My anger builds as Gemma speaks. *She needs to be alone.* Why the hell does Tiba need to be alone? Why won't Gemma tell me what is going on? I pace back and forth in front of the kitchen island. I am about to say something I probably shouldn't say when Raef walks into the room, without Charley this time.

"Tell him, Gemma. Tell him the whole story." Raef stares at Gemma with determination. "He deserves to know."

Gemma's uncertainty shines in her eyes as she holds Raef's gaze. When he reaches her, he rests his forehead on hers, never breaking their connection. After what seems like a lifetime, she finally breaks away and nods. She turns back to me and Raef stays by her side, his arm around her waist.

"I need to know something before I tell you why Tiba left last night. I need to know how you feel about her. Do you love her, Max?" Gemma watches my expression intently. She can read me like a book, so I know I can't lie to her.

"Yes. I do love her." I drag my eyes away from Gemma's and glance at Raef. He smiles at me and gives me a thumbs-up with his free hand. I notice the other one tightens on Gemma. I can't believe I just told them that I love Tiba. Hell, I just realized it myself. Now I have told them instead of Tiba. She should have been the first to know. But if it gets me info on where she is, it will be worth it.

"Okay. We need to sit down. This isn't a short story." Gemma points to the living room. We close the short distance and I sit straight up in the chair I choose. I'm not interested in getting comfortable.

"I'm going to check on Charlotte." Raef kisses the top of Gemma's head as she sits on the couch across from me. He leans down to whisper in her hear and I think I hear the words, "Tell him everything."

Gemma waits until Raef is out of sight before she looks at me. She wrings her hands in front of her. That is her tell when she is nervous. I slide forward on the chair, becoming more anxious to hear what she has to say.

"If I tell you this, I may lose Tiba's friendship forever." Gemma's eyes shine with tears. The motions of her hands even faster now. "She doesn't tell anyone about her past, but you need to know. Especially if you plan to have a future with her."

A future with Tiba. I haven't gotten that far with my plans. Right now, I just want to find her. As I take a moment to think about the future, I can't imagine mine without her in it. I don't say anything, merely tilt my head toward Gemma to let her know I want her to continue.

"I don't know where to begin." Gemma ducks her head. "Tiba came to Granier to hide from her past. When she was 19, she met a guy. He was much older than her, around 30 I think. Anyway, he was in med school and her parents thought he was great. Tiba comes from a family that had always struggled for money, so they saw him as a way for her to have a life they hadn't been able to give her. Everything seemed perfect. Gerard doted on her and Tiba fell in love with him."

Gemma pauses and raises her eyes to meet mine. I clinch my fists when I hear the words *Tiba fell in love with him*. The thought of her being in love with someone else makes me nauseas.

Does she still love him? My gaze holds Gemma's as I look for answers. I manage to mutter, "Continue."

"After about six months, things took a turn. If Tiba did something Gerard didn't like, he would hit her."

Gemma's words are a punch to the stomach. My nausea turns to anger. My clinched fists tighten even more. The muscles in my arms flex. Someone hit my girl. I want to kill him. Before I can say anything, Gemma continues.

"Tiba told her parents after the third or fourth time. They were so wrapped up in the fact Gerard was going to be a doctor that they blew it off. They told her to act better and he would stop. Tiba was heartbroken. Her own parents were siding with a man who abused her. They made it clear that she couldn't come back home if she left him. They wanted her with him, no matter what he did."

"What kind of parents were they?" I ask through gritted teeth. My jaw twitches as I try to control myself.

"The kind that forced their daughter into a horrible position." Gemma stands and walks behind a chair, resting her hands on the back of it. "Tiba stayed with Gerard, even though she didn't want to. She had no money of her own and nowhere to go. Gerard had made her cut off communication with her friends. They only did things with *his* friends. After seeing her parents, things got worse. He was hitting her daily. After one really bad day, Tiba called an old friend of hers after Gerard left the apartment. The friend was a guy, not anyone she had ever dated, just a guy friend. Anyway, he agreed to help Tiba get away from Gerard. He had just gotten to the apartment when Gerard got home. Gerard went off the rails. He pulled a gun from his pants and shot the guy and then beat Tiba until she was unconscious."

"He did WHAT?" I shout as I jump from the couch. My arms shake with anger. I run my hand through my hair while I attempt to comprehend what Gemma has said.

"*Shhh*." Gemma chides me. "Charley can hear you."

"I'm sorry. I can't help it. I want to kill him."

"Let's go outside on the porch. You may have another outburst with the next part of the story." Gemma points to the door.

Outside sounds good to me. I can't seem to breathe inside anyway. Maybe fresh air will help. Gemma sits in the swing when we get to the porch. She motions for me to sit, but I'm too wired. Instead, I pace. Gemma is quiet as she watches me. She allows me time to calm down, but it doesn't work. Finally, I can't take the silence any longer.

"Finish, Gemma."

She nods and continues. "Tiba wound up in the hospital and her friend wound up dead. Her injuries were severe. I don't know the details, but she had a couple of surgeries for internal injuries. They kept her in a medically induced coma for quite some time."

"Did they arrest the idiot that tried to kill her?"

"That's where the story gets more horrifying." Gemma grabs my arm and pulls me to sit in the swing. "Gerard told the police that he walked in and found the guy beating Tiba. He claimed the guy then turned on him. He said he shot him in self-defense. Turns out that Gerard comes from an entrenched crime family in New Orleans. His family had connections to people in the police force, so they bought his story. Tiba's family did too. While she was in a coma, he had nothing to worry about. He was conceited enough that he wasn't worried about anyone finding out the truth. After a couple of weeks, Tiba woke up. She was groggy, but coherent enough to let the nurses know what happened. They called the police and two of them made it to the hospital to take her statement before Gerard came by for the day. Fortunately, it was two good guys. They knew of the history of Gerard's family, so they knew who to talk to and who not to talk to in the department. They put security on Tiba's room and wouldn't allow Gerard in to see her. The next day, they arrested him for murder and attempted murder. Tiba's parents wouldn't believe he did it. They sided with him."

"Fuck!" It's a good thing Gemma brought me outside. There's no way I can hold the anger I feel inside. "What the hell is wrong with those people?" I am off the swing and pacing the length of the porch again.

"I don't know the answer to that." Gemma's tears stream down her face. "Tiba tried to tell them what happened, but they wouldn't listen. They tried to convince her that she had dreamed it while she was in a coma. Even when the police reviewed the evidence and found that it supported Tiba's story, they still wouldn't believe her. When she refused to back down, her parents stopped visiting her in the hospital, even though she was there for almost a month. During that time, Gerard took a plea deal to avoid life in prison."

"At least he's in prison. If he wasn't, I'd have to kill him." Knowing he is behind bars comforts me a little. I lean against a post on the porch.

"Max, what I have to tell you next is going to upset you." Gemma stands and walks in front of me.

"More than what you've already told me? Not likely." I cross my arms across my chest. I can't imagine anything that could upset me more than knowing Tiba almost died at the hands of another man.

"Gerard wasn't just Tiba's boyfriend. He is her husband."

Husband. My chest constricts so tight I think I might pass out. Tiba was married to the asshole. Wait, did Gemma say is? *He is her husband.* Is, not was. Tiba is married. Oh. My. God. Tiba is married. I can't think. I can't breathe. Turning away from Gemma, I bend over, hands on my knees. I attempt to fill my lungs with air. It doesn't work. Gemma's hand is suddenly on my back.

"Max, are you okay?" Gemma leans over to try to see my face, but I can't look at her yet.

"No. I'm not okay." I raise myself back to a standing position, my back still to Gemma. "How could she not tell me she's married?"

"The story doesn't end there, Max. You just needed to know that part before I finish."

"Don't think there's much you can tell me to make this better. Why the hell did she stay married to him? Does she still love him?" That thought has me doubled over again.

"No, she doesn't love him. The day she got out of the hospital, Gerard's brother showed up. He was there to give her a message from Gerard. He told her that he would be watching her for his brother. He would know where she was and who she was with every day. He told her Gerard would never divorce her and she would never be with another man. That if he found her dating someone else,

he would kill him. When he left, Tiba called her
parents to try one more time to get through to
them. She told them what Gerard's brother told
her. They said that she was married to Gerard and
should honor him as her husband. They said that
if she wouldn't stand by him, she couldn't come
home to them. Tiba didn't know what to do. She
was alone and scared with nowhere to go. She
called a friend from high school that had moved to
Granier. She left the city with nothing except the
clothes a nurse bought for her so she could leave
the hospital. She moved out here, started using a
different name, and has been in hiding out here
ever since. She's never dated anyone, only gone
out occasionally with a guy here or there. That's
why she got so upset when she heard what happened at your job site. She has herself convinced
that Gerard's brother did it—or had someone do
it for him—to remind her that she can't be with
anyone."

So many thoughts run through my mind. Tiba is
married because she believed the threats of a man
in prison. Doesn't she know she can divorce him
anyway? She changed her name. I can't get it all
straight in my head. It's too much to comprehend.
I don't say anything because I can't find my voice.
I don't know what I would say if I could.

"See, Max. There's so much more to Tiba than
anyone knows. She's in love with you. She has been
for a long time. She just thinks she can't be with
you. She's going to kill me for telling all of this to
you. Tiba plans on telling you but she wanted to
get her divorce straight first."

Divorce. That gets my attention. I jerk around to

face Gemma.

"She's getting a divorce?"

"Yes. She honestly didn't know she could. She thought it would lead Gerard straight to her. We got Raef and Daniel involved. They didn't know any of her story either. Daniel will handle everything and it all should be final soon. He's also making her name change official."

"Her name. Tiba isn't her name?" It's all I've ever know her as. Now, I realize I don't really know her at all. I don't even know the real name of the woman I have fallen in love with. That realization is overwhelming. "What's her name, Gemma?"

"Henriette Dutillet. Heni for short."

"Henriette. I don't know what to think right now. I don't even know her." My voice is a whisper, both hands in my hair in desperation.

"You do know her, Max. You know Tiba. That's who she is. She's not Henriette any more. She left that girl behind. The strong woman she is today is all Tiba."

"If that's true, why did she run? Why did she run out of my house? She could have told me this and I'd support her. I'd stand by her and help her. Why did she run?" Frustration mounts and I find myself becoming angry at Tiba. Why didn't she trust me?

"She's scared. When you told Tiba what happened at the site, all she could think of was Gerard had found her and was trying to hurt you from prison."

"I'm a big guy. I can protect myself. She should've trusted me." Anger laces my voice.

"I know. And she knows too. She's just scared. Until Daniel gets the legal stuff done, she wants to be gone from this area."

"Where is she? Where did she go, Gemma?"

"She's in Chicago." Gemma twists her hands nervously. "She's with Moss at his home for sex-trafficking victims. It's safe there. No one can get to her."

"With Moss. She can trust him, but she can't trust me." I am full-blown angry now. How could she leave me to run to him?

"Don't be upset. She wanted out of town to protect you as much as herself. Moss provided a safe place for her to stay that she didn't have to pay for. Raef arranged for her to fly to Chicago and Moss picked her up. Please don't be mad at Tiba. She's doing what she thinks is the right thing to do." Gemma pleads with me, but I won't have it. How can I ever trust Tiba if she can't trust me enough to talk to me?

"Stop, Gemma. Just stop. I don't know what the hell to think right now. The woman that I thought I loved doesn't even exist. She's married, and I didn't even know. I didn't know her real name. None of what Tiba and I had was real. None. I can't deal with this. I have to go."

My hands shake from confusion and anger as I dig in my pockets for my truck key. When I reach the bottom of the steps, I stop and turn back to Gemma. Tears continue to fall from her eyes. She loves Tiba like a sister, but she can't convince me that Tiba was right to lie to me.

"Thank you for telling me, Gemma. Thank you for keeping me from making a huge mistake." I turn away and walk to my truck. As I back the truck down the driveway, I see Gemma drop her face into her hands. Her shoulders shake as she cries. I tear my gaze away before I let her emotions get the best of me. I would rather wallow in my anger than let Gemma's tears sway me to forgive Tiba. Not when I finally opened my heart to someone. Not when I was ready to give her all of me.

Chpater 16

TIBA

BORED. THAT'S WHAT I AM, bored. Coming to Chicago was the right thing to do. It got me away from Louisiana and the threat of Gerard. I don't think there is any way he could track me here at the facility Moss has built. He runs this home for victims of sex-trafficking and he goes out of his way to protect the ones that come here. No one gets in this building unless they belong here. But now that I'm here, I'm bored. I miss Granier. It's lonely here.

Granted, I've met several of the girls that currently live here, victims that have been saved. They all have experienced way more trauma than I have, but in a way, we are kindred spirits. We've all suffered at the hands of someone who intended to hurt us. I've even taken Moss up on his offer and spent some time with one of the therapists here. I didn't realize I had so much I needed to work through until the first time I sat down with the psychologist. Now I realize there is much I need to do for myself before I can give all of myself to Max, even if I love him.

I've been here a week now. One week. The

first day, Max texted and tried to call all day, but I didn't answer or return any texts. I couldn't. I didn't know what to tell him. He needed to know about my past, but I couldn't tell him until I knew he was safe.

Gemma called later the first night I was here and told me about her visit from Max. She wound up telling him everything. I was angry at first. It was my place to choose to tell him, not hers. I hung the phone up on her, but after a few minutes, I called her back. Gemma is the one person I can't stay angry with. We spent the next hour crying over the phone with each other. Gemma said he left angry and since that night, he hasn't texted or called. I think it's safe to assume he is done with me.

Glancing at the clock, I notice it is almost seven. I walk into the kitchen of the apartment I occupy and open the refrigerator. Moss had it fully stocked when I arrived. He has made sure I have every-thing I need—and a whole bunch of stuff I don't need.

The fridge contents don't appeal to me tonight. I decide on a glass of wine instead of supper. Maybe I'll sit here and drink myself into oblivion so I won't miss Max so much. I grab a wine glass out of the cabinet and pour it full. Moss has good taste in wine. Every bottle he has for me has been good. So far, I've only tried two bottles. Tonight, I may try the rest. Before I get back to the living room, someone knocks on the door and I change direc-tion to answer it.

Before I open the door, I check the peephole. Outside, Moss holds a wine bottle. Guess we were on the same wavelength tonight. I unlock the two bolts and open the door. He greets me with a huge smile. He notices the wine glass in my hand and holds the bottle in his hand up for me to see.

"Looks like you have a head start on me. I come bearing more."

Stepping back, I let him enter the apartment. He drops a quick kiss on my cheek as he passes. Moss is a hugger and a kisser. It doesn't matter if you are just friends with him, he's still going to kiss you on the cheek, the forehead, the top of the head, or just about anywhere. It put me off a little at first, but I've adjusted to him now and expect it. He's really a great guy, just not the guy for me.

"Grab you a glass and join me. I decided on a wine dinner tonight." I wave my glass in the air. Moss looks over his shoulder and shakes his head.

"We aren't having that. Do you need more groceries?"

"No, Moss. The fridge is full. I just don't feel like cooking and nothing really interested me. Drinking too much wine interests me." I give a wry chuckle. He raises an eyebrow and shakes his head.

"Sounds like someone is having a bad day. How about some pizza? I'll have one delivered from my favorite place. Go sit down and get ready to tell Moss what's wrong." He makes a grand gesture with his arms. I laugh at him but head to the living room. He likes to refer to himself in third person when he tries to cheer someone up. I hear him in the other room on the phone ordering the pizza before he appears in the living room. He drops down into one of the oversized leather chairs in the room and places the wine bottle on the table next to him.

"So, what's got you down, pretty lady?"

My eyes focus on the wine glass in my hand. The wine swirls inside it while I think about how to say what I want to say. I don't want Moss to think I'm ungrateful for his generosity in giving me a place to stay. I pull my legs underneath me and lean against the back of the couch.

"I miss Granier. I miss Gemma and my other friends. I'm so thankful that you let me stay here, but I just miss everyone." The swirl of the wine slows, and I take a sip of it.

"You miss Max." And just like that, Moss gets to the root of the problem.

"Yes."

Moss takes a big drink of his wine. He tilts his head back on the chair and stares at the ceiling. The frown on his face concerns me as he weighs what he is going to say. As much as I miss Max and everyone else, I still need to stay here a little while longer. I hope he doesn't plan to send me back now. I take a deep breath as Moss lifts his head and levels me with his gaze.

"If you love him, call him. I don't know much about you, but I know you have secrets. Hell, we all have secrets. Gemma hasn't told me about your past, but she told me that Max knows. I don't know what you are running from, but if you love Max, don't run from him. Call him and talk to him. Let him know how you feel."

Moss's deep brown eyes never leave mine. I break the connection and drop my gaze back to my glass of wine. The twirling liquid in my hand does nothing to comfort me. When I glance back to him, his arms are on his knees as he leans toward me. He isn't going to let this go without a response.

"I don't know if I can. I don't think I can handle if he rejects me."

"But what if he doesn't? What if he is waiting on you? You won't know unless you try. And if the worst happens, at least you will know."

"You make it sound so easy."

"It is. You're worried about him breaking your heart, but what do you feel now? Wouldn't knowing be better?" Moss finishes his glass of wine and refills it.

"Ugh! I know you're right." I follow his lead and finish my wine, handing it to him to replenish. "I'm just scared." I look at the ceiling after he hands me my wine glass.

"Just try. Promise me."

"Okay, okay. I'll try. He won't answer though. I know him. He won't answer."

That thought makes me sad, but I know Max. He's stubborn. He feels betrayed because I didn't tell him about myself, and now, he will run from me.

"Then you'll keep trying. Call once a day until he answers. Throw in a text if you want to, but call. Every day, call." Moss sips his wine while he watches me. Knowing he won't give in, I finally agree.

"Once a day. No more. Just once a day."

"That's my girl. Hang in there and get your man." He smiles and relaxes in the chair.

"You're pretty good at this relationship stuff. How'd you get so good at advice?"

He visibly stiffens at my question. It's such a fleeting moment, I almost don't catch it.

"Oh, you know, old Moss has some experience with women."

The response is an obvious blow-off of the question, so I decide to push a little more. I am interested in what makes him tick.

"So, no special lady in your life?" I ask. Moss jerks his face toward me then he quickly looks away. His jaw twitches before he gulps the remainder of the wine in his glass.

"Why would I settle for one woman when there are so many out there?" He places his wine glass on the table and stands. His lips are drawn in a tight line across his face as he attempts to smile. "Hate to leave so quickly, but I just remembered that I have some paperwork I need to take care of tonight."

"But you ordered pizza." I'm so shocked by his sudden change in attitude that I don't move from my position on the couch.

"It's paid for. Enjoy it." Moss leans down, drops a quick kiss on my forehead and is gone. I hear the door shut behind him. I'm not sure what just happened, but I evidently hit a touchy subject.

"Well done, Tiba. Run off the person helping you right now." I speak out loud to myself.

Before I can do anything, there is a knock on the door. My first thought is maybe Moss has come back. I rush to the door in hopes that I can apologize for upsetting him. When I throw the door open, I find one of the downstairs security guards holding a pizza.

"Pizza, ma'am." The guard passes the pizza to me.

I mutter a quick, "Thanks" and take the box from him, my disappointment evident. The guard nods before turning back toward the elevator. I throw the pizza on the kitchen counter without opening it. Plopping down in the chair Moss vacated, I fill my wine glass to the top.

"Well, you planned on drinking alone tonight. Looks like you got your wish." I shake my head at myself. I *am* talking to myself. The therapist upstairs will have a hay-day with that.

Thinking about what Moss made me agree to, I pick up my phone. I pull up my text messages, click on Max's name, and reread the messages he sent me before they abruptly stopped arriving. Why didn't I answer any of them? Fear. Fear kept me from responding. Fear drove him away from me. Can I make the move to try to overcome this distance?

Moss is right. I won't know until I try. Before I can change my mind, I click on the buttons necessary to dial Max's number. My stomach churns as his phone rings and rings until his voicemail answers the call. "This is Max. Leave a message."

The sound of his voice makes the distance between us seem even more than it is. It makes me miss him even more. Pressing the end button, I don't leave a message. I was right. I knew he wouldn't answer. At least I tried. I promised Moss once a day. I'll try again tomorrow.

I decide to let Moss know I called so I pull up my last message with him.

I tried to call Max. He didn't answer.

It's only a few seconds before my phone dings with a message from Moss.

Sorry he didn't answer. Try again tomorrow.

Before I can respond to his message, my phone dings again. It's another message from Moss.

Sorry I ran out on you. Wasn't right for me to do that. I don't talk about me so I ran.

I smile sadly at the screen on my phone. Poor Moss, always helping others, but keeps his stuff inside. I type out a message, back it off and just send a simple *Are we okay?*

I watch the dots as he types. Soon his message pops up on the screen.

We are good. Try Max again tomorrow. We'll talk then.
I will. Goodnight Moss.

I toss the phone on the table beside the chair. Moss has been a good friend to me. Maybe he will eventually let me be the same kind of friend to him. Of course, I haven't told him anything about my history, so why should he feel comfortable opening up to me.

Frustrated with myself and my life, I decide to take a long hot bath and try to clear my mind. I grab a piece of pizza out of the box and my glass before I walk into the enormous bathroom. As I fill the tub, I sit on the side eating pizza. I have some decisions to make about how long I plan to stay here. Since I have been drinking wine tonight, I will work on that tomorrow.

Tomorrow. What a big word for me right now. It makes me think of Max. Tomorrow, I will call again. Tomorrow, I will leave a message when he doesn't answer. Maybe.

Chapter 17

MAX

SWING THE HAMMER. DRIVE THE nail. Over and over, I make the motions. It's the only thing that keeps me sane these days. I work alongside the crew daily, not only to keep the job on track for completion by the deadline, but to attempt to handle my irritation with the direction my life has taken. Between the continued vandalism of the jobsite and the complete failure of my personal life, I feel like everything is falling apart. Being able to hit nails over and over releases some of the vexation I feel.

Jerry calls my name and I sit back, wiping the sweat from my forehead. He motions for me to come down to the ground level. I wave back in acknowledgement, drop my hammer into my tool belt, and climb down the ladder.

"What's up?" I ask when I get to the bottom.

"Your ole' man's here to see ya'. We been visitin' but it's time for me to head home to the lil' lady." Jerry's thick accent makes me smile. The love he still has for his wife after many years make me wistful.

"Go home, man. I'll head over to the office and

see Dad." I slap Jerry on the back as I walk by.

When I round the corner, Dad stands in the door of the office building. I wonder why he is here today. He rarely drops by the job just to see me. Heck, he rarely drops by at all. That was the point of me taking over from him. He was ready to retire and not have to be here every day.

"Hey, Dad." I greet him with an extended hand.

"Hello, son." Dad takes my hand but pulls me into a hug. "Job's looking good. Looks like you'll make your completion date."

"If things keep going like they have this week, we will." I motion to the door for him to go inside. "We're still fighting vandalism. Added more cameras the other day, so I hope if they come back, we'll catch 'em."

I drop my tool belt on the desk and flop into the chair behind it. Dad sits across from me, concern etched on his brow.

"Still no clues?" he asks.

"None. They've avoided the cameras every time. It's almost like they know where they are."

"Any possibility of it being the work of one of the crew?"

"Who knows? I do have some new guys on this job due to the size of it. I tried to vet them before hire, but I can't be sure they're all loyal." I rub my hand across my face. I've had the same thought as my father many times over the last few weeks. "The cameras we added this week were all done after hours. No one knows where they are except me and Jerry."

"That's a good approach. Hopefully they won't come back, but if they do, sounds like you're prepared. Still have a guard coming at night?"

"Yes. That's why it's so crazy that someone still manages to wreak havoc here."

"It's a big jobsite, son. If it is someone from the crew, they have inside knowledge of not only how to get in, but how to hide." Dad makes sense. His words convince me that my thoughts of it being an inside job are on track. I just don't know how to figure out who it might be. I certainly can't afford to start laying off people just because I don't know them well. We would never meet the deadline that way.

"Yea, I think you're right. I just don't know how to figure it out." My annoyance with the problem increases when I talk about it, so I change the subject. "So, what brings you by today, Dad?"

"Your mom and I miss you. Thought I would drop by and convince you to come to dinner."

Of course, that's why he's here. I haven't been out to their house in weeks. In fact, I haven't been since before Tiba left town. She's been gone a month and I have had no desire to explain my foul mood to my family, so I've avoided them. Not the most adult way to handle things, but it's worked for me. Until now, that is.

"Sorry, Dad. It's just been a lot going on with the job and all." Deflection. Let's see if that works.

"I know better than that, son. Gemma told us a little about you and Tiba and how Tiba left town."

Well, that answers that. Deflection didn't work. Damn Gemma and her mouth. The last thing I want to do is discuss Tiba with my parents. I fidget with the pen on my desk without looking at my father. He takes my silence as encouragement to continue.

"Your mother is unhappy, and I don't like it. She doesn't deserve to be ignored by her only child." Dad's words are tinged with anger. He is a man who strives to keep his wife happy every day. Obviously, I'm compromising that. He stands and taps on the front of my desk to get my attention. I force my gaze upwards to meet his eyes. "Tonight, you will come to the house for dinner. No excuses."

My dad doesn't issue ultimatums very often, but he just threw one down. He turns and walks out of the office without any further words. Because I respect my parents more than anyone else in the world, I will do as he asks. That means, I will have to suffer through the motherly inquisition. I guess if it makes Mom feel better, I can survive.

After working on some paperwork to clear my mind from Dad's visit, I rise from the chair to go back outside. I remember that I left the area where I worked today quite a mess and want to pick it up before I leave. When I walk out the door of the office, I find the guard assigned for the night. I've become familiar with all of them over the last few weeks.

"Still here?" the guard asks. This one is named Bill and is ex-military. He has a wife and two adorable little girls.

I've spent quite a lot of time visiting with these guys in the evenings. It's kept me from resorting to trips to the bar at night since I promised Jerry that I wouldn't go back to that way of handling my troubles.

"Still here. Had some paperwork to do. But, I've promised my parents that I'll head out to their place for dinner, so I'll be heading out soon. Just got to clean up the mess I left earlier." I wave toward the building in progress.

"Sounds good, man. I'm gonna' check out the perimeter. If I don't see you, have a good night." Bill waves as he turns the opposite direction from where I'm headed.

As I walk back to the ladder, I think about how Dad and I both feel someone on my crew is trying to sabotage this job. I don't know how to dig into the background of any of the workers more than I did before I hired them. It seems like an impossible task. Hopefully the new cameras will do their job. The company used super small cameras this time and they are so discreetly placed that even I sometimes miss them—and I was there when they were installed. In addition, all the cameras record continuously instead of just at night. The extra security is eating into the profits from this job but it's an expense I must absorb right now.

Once I reach the area I need to clean up, I pause to look around. Something seems off, but I can't put my finger on it. I was the only one that worked in this area today, so my stuff is all still scattered across the space. I can't seem to shake the feeling that something isn't right. Moving from room to room on this floor of the building, I don't find anything that looks odd.

Venturing back to the room where I started, I hear a sound behind me. I quickly turn to find nothing. I shake my head in annoyance. I'm letting paranoia invade my mind. The sound was surely on the ground level outside where the guard checks the fence.

While I pick up the stray nails off the floor, my mind wanders to Tiba. She has tried to call me every day for the last three weeks. Once a day, every day. Sometimes I don't know until after she has called, but other times I listen to the phone and let it go to voicemail. Every few days, she will leave a message. "Max, it's Tiba. Please call me so we can talk. I need to tell you some things." It's the same message every time. Some days she will send a text message in addition to the call. The text is always the same as the voicemail.

Gemma has begged me to talk to Tiba. She calls every few days, too. Every time it's to tell me to answer Tiba's calls or to call her back. One or the other. I know I should, and truth be told, I want to. I *want* to talk to Tiba. I just don't think I can. I opened myself to her and she ran from me. She wouldn't even tell me that she was married. Married. I still can't get over that. If only my heart would listen to my head, I would be over this and not stew over her calls every day.

Unfortunately, my stupid heart is still in love with Tiba. All the time I thought I was in love with Gemma, I never felt anything close to the pain I feel now. It's a struggle just to get through the days. Some nights, I find myself with my phone in hand, ready to hit Tiba's number. Each time I stop myself. If she really wants to talk to me, she will come home, and we can talk face-to-face. Until then, I will keep pushing through.

I groan as I think about the night ahead. Having to discuss Tiba is the only reason I've avoided my parents. Mom will want me to talk and then she'll want to give me advice. Dad will quietly listen but will eventually offer his own advice. While I am lost in thought about the upcoming visit, a noise startles me. This time I know it's behind me.

As I turn my head, I catch a glimpse of an arm coming toward me. I feel a hard thud against the side of my head and suddenly I'm falling. Before I land, everything goes dark.

Chapter 18

TIBA

THROUGH THE FOG OF SLEEP, I hear music. At first, I think it's part of a dream, but it stops and starts again. I force myself awake when I realize the music comes from my phone. It's the ringtone I have for Gemma. When I glance at the clock on the nightstand, I see it's still the middle of the night. My heartbeat quickens as I grab the phone. Gemma would only call me at this time of the night if something is wrong.

Just as I hit the answer button, I hear someone banging on the apartment door. I jump out of my bed and put the phone to my ear.

"Gemma, what's wrong?" I don't waste time with pleasantries. There is no doubt in my mind that something has happened.

"You have to come home, Tiba. Now. It's Max. He's been injured." Gemma's voice is laced with the tears. Her words stop me in my tracks.

Fear races through my body like a bolt of lightning. Before I can ask questions, the banging begins again at my door. I take the final few steps and throw open the door. Moss stands on the other side, one hand on his hip, the other in his hair. His eyes are filled with concern.

"Is that Gemma?" Moss asks as he pushes past me into the apartment.

"Tiba! Are you there? Did you hear me? You need to come home *now*." Gemma's voice rings in my ear at the same time Moss questions me.

"I'm here. I'm here. What happened? Is Max okay?" I whisper into the phone.

"Moss will tell you everything. He's going to bring you home. Don't waste time on the phone with me. Just get here." I've only heard fear in Gemma's voice like this one other time when Charley was kidnapped by Raef's father.

"Moss is here. Please tell me if Max is okay. Please tell me he's alive." My worst fear grasps my heart like a fist squeezing a ball. I can't breathe waiting on her answer.

"He's alive. It's bad but he's holding his own right now. Just get here, okay? He needs you. *I* need you." Gemma's voice catches with a sob.

"I'll be there. I'll be there just as soon as I can." I look around and see Moss has walked into my bedroom. I follow and find him in my closet, pulling out my suitcase.

"Be safe, Tiba. I love you." The phone goes dead.

I am rooted in one spot with a thousand thoughts jumbled in my mind. Max is hurt and I'm not there. Moss has my suitcase open and is right in front of me. He reaches out and grabs both of my arms.

"Tiba. Get it together. We've got a plane waiting on us." He leads me to the closet when I don't move on my own. "Throw some clothes in your bag. We need to go now."

A tear escapes the corner of my eye. I drop my

head and suck in a breath. *Get it together, Tiba. Max needs you.* The little voice in my head gets my attention. I raise my eyes to Moss and take one more deep breath.

"Give me five minutes."

Moss nods in agreement and I grab some clothes from the closet. I don't look at what I pack, I just throw things in the bag. Realizing I have on pajamas, I grab some yoga pants and a t-shirt out of the dresser drawer before I run to the bathroom. I change quickly, throwing my makeup and hair supplies in a bag I pull from under the counter. A quick glance in the mirror lets me know that even though I am dressed, I am quite a sight. My hair is crazier than normal. The tight lines on my face would let anyone see that I'm about to break down.

By the time I'm out of the bathroom, Moss has moved the suitcase to the other room. He stands with one hand on the doorknob and the other holding my purse. I slide my feet into the shoes that sit beside the door. "I'm ready. Let's go."

He grabs the bag I have and hands me my purse. He reaches down and picks up my camera bag and throws it over his shoulder. I didn't notice it beside him before. Moss motions for me to walk ahead of him when he opens the door. I hit the down button on the elevator and we wait. It seems to take forever for it to arrive on my floor, even though it was only a few seconds.

Once inside the elevator, I turn to face Moss. "You said there's a plane waiting for us?" I ask him.

"Yes. I have a friend that owns a plane. I called him, and his pilot will be ready for take-off as soon as we get there." The doors open as we reach the bottom floor. Moss nudges me forward. "I've got a car waiting at the curb."

He moves in front of me as we exit the building. Sure enough, a black limousine sits right outside the front doors of the building. The doorman grabs the bags from Moss and heads to the back of the car. He stows them away while I climb into the back of the vehicle. Moss says a few words to the doorman, shakes his hand and jumps into the seat beside me.

"Quickest route to the airport," Moss tells the driver.

"Yes, sir." The driver pulls onto the road and we are on our way.

Moss turns sideways in the seat and takes my hand in his.

"You're shaking." His brow furrows. "Are you cold?"

"No. Worried. What happened, Moss? What happened to Max?" My voice quivers.

"I don't know all the details, but someone jumped Max at the job site. He was hit in the head with a piece of pipe and pushed from the second floor."

Gasping from what Moss says, the image of Max being attacked flashes through my mind. Who could have done such a thing? Daniel and Raef have assured me that Gerard was not going to do anything to get at me. Even his brother is in prison now. Were they wrong and this is really Gerard's work? The thought makes me shake even harder. I rub one arm with the other to calm myself.

"Do they know who did it?" *Please don't let this be my fault.*

"Not yet. But they have video. Max just had more cameras put up at the site. The security company is reviewing the feed now. By the time we get there, they should know more." Moss glances down at his phone as if he expects to see a message or call. He looks back up and straight into my eyes. "I told Gemma to call or text as soon as she hears something."

Nodding, I pull my eyes from Moss's gaze. When we land in New Orleans, I may find out that my past is responsible for Max's injuries. Will I be able to live with myself if the reason he is hurt is my fault? And if it was the work of Gerard, will someone be waiting to hurt me?

"How bad is it? A fall like that is bad, right?" I ask as my fingers run back and forth on the edge of my shirt.

"I don't know. The security guard was hit from behind and was knocked out too. He thinks he was only out for a few minutes. When he came to, he contacted the police and waited at the gate for them. When the police arrived, one took the guard's statement and the other two searched the job site. That's when they found Max. They think he was attacked first and the guard was hit when the person was trying to get out."

"Is he going to be okay?"

"I don't know, Tiba. I won't lie to you and tell you he will when I don't know." Moss squeezes my hand. "He's not conscious right now, but they've airlifted him to New Orleans and he has the best doctors in the state working on him."

Moss's response does nothing to comfort me. I appreciate that he isn't leading me to believe something that might now be true, but some encouragement right now would go a long way. Instead, he continues to hold my hand in comfort and let my thoughts percolate in my head. I'm so deep inside my mind, worried about Max, worried that this could be my fault, that I don't realize we are at the airport until Moss gets my attention.

"We're here. Are you okay?" Moss has one hand on the side of my face and stares at me with concern in his eyes. "I couldn't get you to come back to me just then."

"Sorry. I was lost in my thoughts." I motion to the door. "Let's go."

He nods but continues to frown. He exits the car and helps me out. The driver already has our bags to the plane and transferred to someone who loads them. When we reach the top of the stairs to the plane, Moss introduces me to the pilot. I barely acknowledge the man, but he doesn't seem to mind. The sound of Moss and the pilot discussing the trip drones on in my ears without me listening to their words. My mind is already in New Orleans with Max.

Moss and the pilot finish their conversation. The pilot moves on to the cockpit and we get settled into seats on a couch. Moss buckles me in before he does himself. I glance around the area and realize we are in a very fancy plane. Any other time, I would be reveling in flying in such an impressive aircraft, but today it's merely a means to an end, getting me from point A to point B.

Once in the air, the flight attendant asks if we want anything. Moss asks for a drink. I don't say anything. I hear him tell her to bring me a water. I

don't want water. I want to be at the hospital with
Max. I unbuckle myself and slide to the end of the
couch, curling my body into a tight ball in the corner. When the attendant returns, Moss holds out
the bottle of water to me. Not wanting to hurt his
feelings, I accept it and place it the cup holder on
the arm of the couch.

"You want to catch a quick nap?" he asks.
"There's a bedroom in the back." He points to the
back of the plane.

Shaking my head, I know I can't sleep. My worry
is too great. I just need to see Max. Maybe when I
can lay my eyes on him, I'll feel better. Hopefully
he'll be awake by the time we land. What if he is
and doesn't want to see me? As long as he is okay,
I can live with that. I will stay in the waiting room
if he doesn't want me in his room. Just so I'm close
to him.

Moss seems to pick up on my silence and doesn't
try to talk to me. He moves to a chair on the other
side of the plane and pulls out his phone. I raise an
eyebrow his direction.

"Plane has wifi," he says as he shrugs his shoulders.

I nod and lay my head on the arm of the couch.
My mind swarms with thoughts of Max. The last
few weeks, I've tried to contact him every day, just
like I promised Moss. Some days I would try to
call and send a message. I haven't gotten any type
of response from him during that time.

Maybe I should have just gone home after Daniel finished with my divorce. He had it and my
official name change done in record time. It's been
my choice to stay on in Chicago. The therapist I've

been seeing at Moss's place is helping me so much, I felt my best option was to stay. Now, though, I wonder what would have happened if I had gone straight back home once I found out I was safe from Gerard.

Safe. A word I haven't embraced in years. Am I really safe now? Is Max? Did someone Gerard knows do this to Max? So many questions. Raef hired a private investigator who reported that Gerard's brother is in prison, so I know it wasn't him, but maybe there is someone else out there.

When Daniel and Raef met with Gerard in prison, they said he was very cordial to them. He claimed he regretted what he had done to me and would never try to harm me again. They talked to the warden and verified that Gerard has received extensive psychological help since he has been incarcerated. The warden also said that Gerard has found religion and was the regular leader of the prison chapel. I want to believe this turn of events with Max has nothing to do with him, but the fear that has haunted me over the years makes me scared it does.

Right now, who did it isn't my main concern. Max's health is. He's got to be okay. I can't even imagine if he's not. I haven't had the chance to tell him that I love him. *He'll be okay. He'll be okay.* The words play over and over in my mind.

A noise startles me and I jerk to a sitting position. I realize I dozed off on the arm of the couch. A quick look around tells me that the noise was Moss. He's clicking his seatbelt into place.

"Buckle up. We're landing." Moss hands me the strap for my seat.

"We're home? Already?" Although I know the flight is only a couple of hours, I'm still shocked to find out that we have made it.

"Yep. We're home. Raef's at the airport waiting on us." Moss smiles in my direction. "We'll have you to Max in no time."

"Any news from Gemma?"

"Raef said they don't know anything new."

The lights on the ground get closer and closer as we land. I dig around in the corner of the couch and find my phone to see what time it is. The glowing screen tells me it's almost 3 A.M. Under normal circumstances I would think the view from the plane window was beautiful. There is nothing normal about this trip home and my thoughts are more about Max than enjoying the scenery.

The landing goes smoothly, and we quickly exit the plane. Raef waits at the bottom of the stairs, just as Moss said he would. I rush down the steps and he envelopes me into a hug. Tears stream down my cheeks as holds me.

"Gem and I are so glad you are here." Raef pulls back from me and I see how deeply the events of the day have affected him. There are dark circles under his eyes and his hair is crazy from him obviously running his hands through it over and over. Moss and Raef shake hands before guiding me toward Raef's car.

"I wish I could've gotten here sooner. Any news from the hospital?"

"Gemma said there has been no change. Max is still unconscious. They are monitoring him closely right now for brain swelling. So far so good though."

"What's the extent of his injuries?" Moss questions as Raef drives us out of the airport. It shocks me that there is little traffic but then I remember that we are in the wee hours of the morning.

"His right side is pretty banged up. He has a broken hip and leg. The leg is broken in multiple places. That's the side he landed on, so it took the brunt of the fall. His arm is bruised and swollen, but miraculously it didn't have any breaks." Raef's eyes find mine in the rear-view mirror as he pauses. He holds my gaze only for a moment before he looks back at the road. It's just long enough for me to see the immense amount of concern in them. "The main worry right now is his head. He was hit with a pipe on the side of his head and then had the other side of it hit when he landed from the fall. They've checked for bleeds and thankfully he has none. Now it's pretty much a waiting game until he wakes up to know what kind of damage was done. The docs say it could be significant or it could be none."

My heart sinks with Raef's words. I don't even want to think about the possibility of Max having a brain injury. He is such a strong hardworking guy. A brain injury that would keep him down would be devastating to him.

"Have they done surgery to fix the hip?" Moss continues to ask questions that my mind can't seem to come up with.

"Not yet. They said it isn't necessary to do surgery immediately and they don't want to put him under anesthesia until they see if there will be brain swelling. The first twenty-four hours is a critical time."

Critical. That word catches my attention and I snap my eyes back to the mirror where I see Raef once again glance at me. *Critical.* Raef's voice plays over and over in my mind.

"Is Max going to make it?" I ask in a whisper.

"Umm . . . " Raef hesitates before he answers. "The docs think he will, but they can't say for sure. With a head injury there is always a risk. We just need to get through the next few hours."

More tears pour from my eyes. Max can't die. He just can't. I lay my head against the back of the seat of the car. Memories of the short time I had with Max play in my mind like a video on repeat. Every moment seems even more significant now. Moss and Raef continue to talk in the front seat but I don't listen to what they say.

The trip to the hospital is made in record time even though it feels like it takes forever. Raef drops us off at the emergency entrance before he heads to the parking garage. As I stand in front of the sliding doors, I find myself rooted in place. Moss realizes I am no longer beside him and turns back to find me staring at the doors.

"Tiba, are you okay?" Moss asks as he grips my shoulders with his hands.

"I don't know if I can go in there," I say quietly. "What if he dies, Moss? What if Max doesn't make it?"

"*Shh.* He's going to be alright. He's a tough guy. Let's go in. I'll be here with you and Gemma is inside those doors. She needs you right now too." Moss squeezes my shoulders and then moves one hand to my elbow. He moves beside me and gently eases me forward. I follow his lead and we pass through the emergency room doors.

As soon as we are in the waiting room, I see Gemma. She spots us and runs straight to me, throwing her arms around me. She holds me so tightly I almost can't breathe.

"Thank God you're here!" Gemma exclaims. She doesn't let go of me, instead clings to me as if I may disappear. I don't say anything, just hold her in a vice-grip quite like she holds me. Gemma's tears are wet against my cheek as they mix with my own. After several minutes of this, we finally pull away from each other.

Her eyes are red, and her face is swollen from crying. Her hair is in a bun with pieces slipping out all over. Worry is etched in her features. Her eyes shine with fear. She gives Moss a quick hug, thanks him for getting me here so quickly, and then grabs my hand.

"They've moved Max to ICU. Everyone else is in the waiting room upstairs. I stayed down here to wait on you. Let's get up there." Gemma pulls me behind her toward the hall.

"I'll wait down here for Raef and then we'll come up," Moss calls out to us. I'm not sure Gemma hears him as she trots down the hall with me in tow.

We take the elevator and make quick work of getting upstairs. When we enter the waiting room, Max's mother jumps from her chair and meets us at the door. She grabs me into a hug with Jack right behind her to do the same.

"Oh, Tiba. I'm so glad you're here. Our boy is hurt." The normally unflappable Kathleen is in pieces. Jack wraps an arm around her and pulls her closer to him. She rests her head against him.

"I'm so sorry, Kathleen. I know you and Jack are so worried. Any news?"

"Nothing new. They have him on all sorts of monitors. Just a waiting game now." Jack guides Kathleen back to a chair. She all but falls into it and he quickly sits beside her, pulling her back into his arm. "There isn't another visiting time until six but the nurses up here are great. They said you can have a quick visit since you haven't had a chance to see him."

Fear grabs me like a choke-hold on my heart. I want to see Max, but I'm scared to see him. Not knowing what to expect, I know that I don't want to go in alone. I grab Gemma's hand and hold it tightly.

"Can Gemma go in with me?" My eyes dart from Jack to Gemma.

"I'm sure they won't mind." Jack extricates his arm from Kathleen. "Baby, I'm going to walk the girls to the ICU door so they can see our boy. You'll be okay for a few minutes, won't you?" Jack caresses Kathleen's cheek with the back of his hand. The worry in his eyes is not only for his son but for his wife also. She leans into his hand and nods. He kisses her forehead before standing.

"Come on girls," he says quietly. He glances over his shoulder at Kathleen before he moves through the door. "I don't want to leave Kathleen alone for long. She isn't handling this too well."

Gemma grabs Jack's arm as we walk down the hall. "Max is her only child. No one can expect her to hold up too well in a situation like this."

"You're right, Gem. I'm just not used to seeing

her like this. She's usually so strong. I'm worried about Max, but I'm worried about her too." Jack sighs. He ducks his head as a tear escapes his eye. He hastily wipes it away. "It's all almost too much."

As we stop outside the ICU doors, Gemma hugs Jack. His arms wrap around her and I stand aside to allow them a moment. Jack is like a father to Gemma and I know he feels the same for her. He's being strong for Kathleen, but you can see the stress on his face, taught with tension. He looks at the ceiling and takes a deep breath before easing away from Gemma. Jack knocks lightly on the door and in moments a nurse appears through the doorway.

"Mr. Greenwood. What can we do for you?" the nurse asks. Since she calls him by name, I assume this is one of the nurses he had spoken to earlier.

"How's my boy?"

"About the same. He's holding his own." The nurse smiles as she pats his arm.

"That's good news. He's a strong young man." Jack nods in my direction. "This is the young lady I told you about. Can she and Gemma have a minute with Max? Tiba just got in from Chicago."

"Of course. We can't let them stay for long, but we don't mind if they come in for a few minutes."

"Thanks. I'm going to get back to my wife. Let us know if there are any changes."

"Will do, Mr. Greenwood." The nurse turns to us as Jack walks away. "Come on in ladies." She steps aside and lets us through the door.

The first thing I notice is the quietness of the area. There is no noise except the occasional beep from a machine somewhere in the distance. There are a few people behind the counter at the nurse's station. They offer kind smiles as we pass them. My stomach churns with nervousness as we arrive at Max's room.

"You can have a few minutes with him. He's still unconscious but feel free to talk to him. We actually encourage it." The nurse eases the curtain open and walks into the space.

There are wires everywhere, and I gasp when I see Max. His leg is some type of large splint. His swollen face is black and blue. My hand covers my mouth as the tears fall. He looks so helpless, not the strapping guy I am so used to seeing. His large frame takes up most of the bed but the machines that surround him diminish his size.

The nurse checks the monitors before turning to leave us. When she notices my distress, she gently gives my shoulder a pat. "He's really doing well considering what happened," she says as she passes through the curtain.

Gemma has moved into the semi-dark room and is next to the bed. She quietly talks to Max and holds his hand. I convince myself to move beside Gemma. She brings my hand in to replace hers. The warmth of his hand comforts me. It tells me that he is most definitely alive, even if he doesn't look like he is.

I move closer to Max's head when Gemma backs away from the bed. She gives me a nod and walks out of the room. Even though I thought I didn't want to do this alone, I am grateful that she is giving me this time alone with Max.

"Hey, big guy." Still holding his hand, I take my other hand and touch his swollen, bruised cheek. "Not sure what to think of you jumping out of buildings these days." I joke even though I don't feel like laughing. In case he can hear me inside his head, I want to keep things light.

"They tell me you won't wake up. You can sleep now, but we need you to wake up soon. I've got so much to tell you." I pause and take a much-needed deep breath. I keep looking at Max like he is going to wake up and respond, when I know that isn't going to happen. "There's one thing I want to tell you right now though."

My hand on his cheek stills and I lean further over the bed to get closer to him. My head hovers near his as I whisper the words, "I love you, Max Greenwood. I love you with everything I have in me. You've got to fight through this and wake up, so I can say those words when you are awake."

Just as I place a light kiss on his lips, the nurse comes back in the room to tell me it's time to go. I squeeze Max's hand one more time before I slide mine from his. With one last look at the sleeping giant I love, I follow the nurse out of his room. Tears fall faster than I can wipe them away.

Now we wait. We wait for Max to come back to us. I wait for him to come back to me.

Chapter 19

MAX

BEEP. BEEP. BEEP. WHAT IS that incessant noise? Beep. Beep. Beep. Whispers of voices sound so far away. *We've changed the IV, so the beeping will stop now.* Who said that? Quiet. No beeping. I like that. Whoever said that is my hero right now. I like the quiet. I'll just open my eyes and see who it was. Wait, why won't my eyes open? Am I dreaming? That's it, I'm asleep.

Voices. I hear more voices. It sounds like Mom and Dad. Why are they whispering? And why are they at my house when I'm asleep? I need to get out of bed to see what they're doing here. Why won't my eyes open? I want them to open. Maybe I just need to rub the sleep off of them. I try to raise my right arm, but nothing happens but pain. Wow! I must have slept on that arm all night for it to hurt like that. I lift my left arm toward my face but is seems like it weighs a ton and it drops onto my chest.

"Jack! Jack! He moved his arm! Max moved his arm!" I hear my mother's voice exclaim. What the hell is she talking about, and again, why are they at my house?

"Max, son. Come back to us. Try to wake up now?" My dad's voice is low but echoes through my brain. This must be one intense dream.

Trying again, I manage to get one eye cracked enough to see the shine of a bright light. I immediately close it tightly, scrunching my face from the light. Picking my arm up again, I manage to get it to my eyes. I let it fall over them instead of rub them like I want to. Someone grabs my hand and moves my arm away from my face.

"Oh, Max! Please wake up for us!" My mom's voice encourages me to try to open my eyes again. I really want to know what is going on here.

After straining and straining, I manage to get both eyes to crack open at the same time. I turn my head toward the area I think the voices have been coming from and am hit with a sudden sharp pain that radiates through my entire head. It takes my breath away and I close my eyes again. When the pain dulls to a throb, I open them. The first thing I see is my parents leaning over a railing with their eyes locked on my face.

"You're awake! Oh, my sweet baby boy, you are awake!" My mom grabs both sides of my face and kisses my forehead.

"Welcome back, son. You had us worried." Dad's voice booms and he too leans over the rail to kiss me.

I can see around them enough to know that I'm not in my house. I'm not in their house either. So, the question becomes, where am I? And why does my head hurt so bad? And why can't I lift my right arm? Something has happened, but I have no idea what. I open my mouth to speak but no words come out.

"Jack, run get the nurse. They need to know he's awake."

Dad reaches across the bed and grips my hand before quickly turning away. I hear the soft closure of the door as he leaves the room. I open my mouth again to speak, but still nothing. I try to clear my throat and manage to get a groan out.

"*Shhh.*" Mom pushes my hair back from my face. "Don't rush it. You've been through a lot."

What does she mean I've been through a lot? I want to know where I am and what's wrong with me. I clear my throat again and this time it brings on a cough. The knifelike pain shoots through my head again and I roll it back to where I face the ceiling of the brightly lit room. Man, that pain is tough. After a few moments, it again dulls to a throb. Without moving my head to look back toward my mother, I open my mouth and try one more time to speak.

"Where am I?" I manage to get out in a croak-like whisper.

"Oh, Max! You're in the hospital. Don't you remember what happened?"

I move to shake my head, but that brings on the pain so I quickly stop and muster up a "no."

"You were attacked at the job almost three weeks ago. You've been unconscious since then. We were so worried!" I can hear the tears in my mom's voice, so I turn my head to look at her, even though the pain is almost unbearable. I need to see her face. Sure enough, tears pour down her cheeks.

Before I can try to comfort her, I hear the door open and footsteps approach the bed. I know better than to try to lift my head to look, so I wait until they reach me.

"Well, hello there, Mr. Greenwood. Glad to have you back with us." A nurse in blue scrubs stands by the bed. She reaches for the machine next to me and presses a button. I feel something tighten on my arm and she moves to put a thermometer in my mouth. "Just getting some vitals on you now that you're awake."

The next few minutes are spent with the nurse as she checks me over and records things into a laptop. She asks questions and I try to respond to the yes and no questions as best I can without moving my head too much. I manage to get the words out each time, but it is exhausting. Once she is done, she leaves the room and lets us know the doctor will be in soon.

With everything quiet again, Mom and Dad come back to the side of the bed. Now I can get some answers on how I was attacked. I don't remember anything after promising Dad that I'd go to the farm for dinner.

"What happened?" I whisper. Dad pulls a chair over to the side of the bed and sits next to me. Mom lowers the side rail and sits beside me on the bed, never loosening her hold on my hand.

"According to the guard, you went upstairs at the job to clean up after I left that day. He went on about his check of the exterior fence until he heard a crash. He turned and was punched in the face and knocked out. After the police came, they found you where you had fallen through a window and landed on a stack of materials that had not been unwrapped. That's what kept your injuries from being worse; you didn't fall all the way to the ground." Dad pauses and wipes a stray tear from his eye. My father is one of the strongest men I know, so to see him with even one tear lets me know this was pretty serious.

"What injuries?" It's crazy that I don't even know what's wrong with me. Mom squeezes my hand and I turn my gaze toward her.

"You landed on your right side and broke your hip and leg. Obviously, that hit first because you didn't break your arm, just bruised it pretty badly. You were hit on the head with a pipe before the fall, and then hit the other side of your head when you landed. You had some brain swelling but fortunately it didn't get to the point that they had to do anything to relieve the pressure. It resolved on its own pretty quickly." Tears cover my mother's cheeks. "You scared us so much, Max. The swelling in your brain went down but you wouldn't wake up. We didn't know if you would or not."

Mom kisses my hand and holds it to the side of her face. I feel the dampness of her tears against my fingers. My mind tries to process what she said about my injuries. My head is fuzzy and with the incessant dull throbs, it doesn't all seem to register to me. I'm not sure what it means for me now.

"Am I okay?"

"You're awake and that's a good thing." I hear from across the room. I turn my head slightly, ignoring the pain, and see who I assume is my doctor walk toward my bed. "How do you feel?"

"Like I've been hit by a truck."

"You'll probably feel that way for a while. Can you tell me your name?"

"Max Greenwood."

"Good. I'm going to ask you some questions that may sound silly, but I need to check your memory since you did have a significant head injury."

Instead of nodding or responding, I give the doctor a thumbs-up. He proceeds to ask me various things like my birthday, where I live, who's the president, what are my parent's names and more. It seems to go on forever and my throat gets scratchy, but my voice gets stronger as I answer. After what seems like fifty stupid questions, the doctor asks me if I remember what happened to me.

"No. Nothing. My parents told me, but that's all I know."

"That's not unusual with a head injury like yours." The doctor pulls out a pen light and shines it in my eyes, one at a time. "You may never remember that day. That's the way it plays out with many traumatic brain injuries."

"Is that what I had? A traumatic brain injury?" That sounds terrible and suddenly I find myself more worried than I was before.

"Yes, you did. Anytime there is brain swelling with a significant head injury, that's what it is. You don't seem to have any lasting effects from it, other than the memory loss from the incident."

"Is that why my head hurts so bad when I move it?"

"Absolutely. And it will for some time. You'll probably feel a dull ache for several days, even weeks. You took quite a lick to both sides of your head. We can give you something to help with that pain now that we've assessed you. Your orthopedic doctor will be in later today to discuss getting you out of this bed and walking. He'll also want to talk to you about physical therapy. As far as I'm concerned, I'd like to watch you another couple of days here in the hospital, but barring any problems, I'll be ready to release you from my care here. It will be up to the ortho after that."

The doctor turns toward my father and shakes his hand then reaches across my bed to hold my mother's hand. "You have your son back. Let me know if he has any odd behavior but I don't expect him to. I think he is going to be just fine."

After he shakes my hand, the doctor leaves the room. I hear a rustle at the door as he leaves and lift my head to see what's going on. Searing pain shoots through it and I drop back to the pillow just in time to hear a screech.

"He's awake!" The screech obviously comes from Gemma. She runs to the side of the bed and appears in front of my eyes. "Oh my God! You're awake!"

"I am, and you're screeching in my ear."

"Oh! I'm sorry!" Gemma's tones her voice down. Just as she does, I see another face appear beside hers.

Tiba. Tiba stands by Gemma, beside my bed. Seeing her feels like a fist around my heart. When did she get here? Better yet, why is she here? Even though it hurts, I turn my head away from her. I can't look at her right now, even though I want to drink in the sight of her. I still have too many questions about my health to deal with the emotions she brings.

When Gemma realizes why I turned my head, I hear her intake of breath. She whispers something, but I can't hear her. I assume she is talking to Tiba. My mother's eyes dart from me to Gemma and Tiba then back to me. It's apparent she doesn't know what to do, so I decide to make it easy for her. "I'd like some rest. Could everyone leave me alone for a while?"

Mom jumps into action.

"Of course, son. Girls do you mind? Max has to be exhausted with the doctor and all. Let's give him some time." She *shoos* them toward the door with her hands.

"No problem. Get some rest, Max." Gemma pats my arm on her way out. "I'm so glad you're awake."

Tiba says nothing. The next sounds come from the door as it opens and then closes. Everyone is gone except my mom. She sits back down on the side of the bed next to me in the same position she was earlier.

"I'm going to stay with you. I finally have you back. Do you mind?"

"Of course not, Mom. I just couldn't handle the girls right now. You understand that right?"

"I do. I'm sure it was a shock to see Tiba. You've been through so much and had no idea they were about to walk in."

"When did she get here?"

"Tiba? She came in the night it happened. Gemma called her right after she found out, and she got here as soon as she could. Son, Tiba hasn't left the hospital since she got here. Gemma brings her clothes every day. If she isn't in this room, she is no farther than the waiting room or the coffee shop." Mom reaches over and touches my cheek. "That girl loves you. I know now isn't the time, but the time will come soon that you two will have to talk. For now, you rest."

Tiba hasn't left the hospital. I've been here almost three weeks and she hasn't left the hospital. That doesn't make sense to me. She left me, so why would she sit here at this hospital with me? Maybe she feels guilty for leaving. Maybe my attack had something to do with her husband. I haven't asked if they knew who did it. It's all too much for me right now. I fade off to sleep with images of Tiba in my mind.

Chapter 20

TIBA

HE'S AWAKE! MAX IS FINALLY awake. I'm so relieved, even if he did turn his head away when he saw me. Then he made it clear he didn't want me there by asking everyone to leave. I know that was directed to me, but I accept it and will do as he wishes . . . for now. Gemma and I make our way down the hall to the waiting area in silence. Fortunately, no one is in the room when we get there. We have our little area set up in the corner of the room with blankets and books. I have spent every night in this waiting room except for the few nights that I've stayed in Max's room to give his parents a break.

"Isn't it wonderful that Max is awake?" Gemma brings me back to the present as we sit in our corner.

"It is, Gem! I hate that I made him uncomfortable though."

"Don't stress over it. He'll get past that. Just give him a little time. You haven't seen each other in forever."

"I know. I'm not going to pressure him to talk to me right now. I've waited this long to tell him how

I feel, I can wait a little longer."

"Hang in there. It really is all going to be okay.
The main thing is that he's awake now. Everything
else will work itself out. Do you want to go to the
loft and get some rest now that he's awake?"

Gemma has pushed me for days to get out of the
hospital. Raef still has a loft in the city and she has
offered it to me time and again. Moss offered me
his place and even left me a key to it when he flew
back to Chicago. They just don't understand that
I can't leave. I walked away from Max once and I
will not leave this hospital until I tell him how I
feel. I will not leave until he knows just how much
I love him, regardless of how he feels. I will not
leave until he is released to go home.

"Gemma, you know I'm not going to leave the
hospital. If Max is here, I'm here."

"I know. I know. I just thought I'd try. You need
more rest than you get here."

"I'm fine. I get a few hours of sleep a day. I can
get a decent meal here. And they have a 24-hour
coffee shop. What more can a girl ask for?" I curl
up in the chair and pull a blanket over my legs.
"This is home for now."

"Okay, I'll drop it. How about I go out and get
us some food? We can have something other than
hospital food today."

"Sure, girlie. Surprise me with something. I think
I'll take a quick nap."

"Sounds good. I'll be back shortly." Gemma
grabs me in the chair and hugs me. "It's all going
to be okay."

Before she gets on the elevator, Gemma looks
over her shoulder one last time and waves to me

through the glass. That girl is my family and I am so thankful for her, even when she hovers over me and tries to mother me.

Thankful for a moment alone, I rest my head on the back of the chair. I see Jack pace in the hall on his cell phone. I'm sure he has many calls to make to let everyone know Max is awake. *Max is awake.* I say it in my mind over and over. For so many days, I didn't know if he would ever wake up. Now he has. I close my eyes for a moment. Maybe I can catch a little nap after all.

Something brushes my arm and I hear my name in the distance. I jerk awake to find Jack in the chair next to me. Wild eyed, I realize I must have fallen into a deep sleep.

"Hey. It's okay. It's just me." Jack squeezes my arm again.

"How long have I been asleep?" I run my hands over my hair and push it out of my face.

"About four hours."

"What?!" I sit upright in the chair. Four hours? That can't be right!

"You were resting so well we didn't want to bother you." Jack chuckles. "I hated to wake you now, but I finally talked Kathleen into leaving the hospital to get something to eat and I was hoping to get you to sit with Max until we get back."

My eyes jump to meet Jack's. I search for something in them to tell me if Max is okay with this or not. I don't get the answer I want.

"Does Max know this?"

"Um, no." Jack's eyes dart from mine as he shifts uncomfortably in his chair. "But after they gave him some pain medicine and he napped, he seems more himself. If you don't want to, I understand." Jack stands and looks out the window of the waiting room. I follow him up and put my hand on his arm.

"Of course, I will do it. I know Kathleen needs a break. And you know I need to talk to Max anyway. This will be as good of a time as any, right?"

Jack lets go of a deep breath. His shoulders sag in relief. For the first time in days, I take a long look at him and realize how much this situation with Max has aged him. He has dark bags under his eyes from lack of sleep. His hair is longer than normal, and he looks like there are some new wrinkles on his face. He breaks into a smile and grabs me into one of his big Jack Greenwood hugs.

"Thank you, Tiba. I just need to get my wife out of here for a little while." Jack pulls back with his hands on my shoulders. "And you talk some sense into that boy of mine. Now that I know he's going to be okay, I'm ready for the two of you to work out your problems."

"I don't know if that will happen or not, but I do love your son. And I'm going to tell him that. Just know that no matter how Max responds, I'll still be there for him. I'll help you and Kathleen in any way I can with his recovery."

"I know you will. That boy loves you. He's a bit stubborn, but he does love you. Thank you again, Tiba. For everything. For staying here and being here for us and Max." Jack gives me another quick hug and grabs the doorknob to the waiting room exit. "I'm going to go get Kathleen. Gemma left you some food earlier. If you want to eat before you go in, that's fine. Max will be fine alone for a bit."

"I'll save it for later. I'm not hungry right now anyway. Just give me a minute to straighten up my stuff in here and I'll be in."

After Jack leaves the room, I fold my blanket and stack it back in the corner. I notice the plate of food that Jack said Gemma brought. I can't stomach anything with the thought of what I'm about to do. The idea of spilling my guts to Max makes me queasy. I make quick work of putting the food in the small refrigerator kept in the waiting room for the patients' families to use. It's time to get down the hall to Max's room.

Chapter 21

MAX

"GO ON, MOM. I'LL BE fine."
My mother hovers over me while my
dad tries to pull her out the door. She nervously
pulls up the blanket on my bed. Dad picks up her
purse and gently holds her hand while she waivers
back on forth on her decision to leave.

"I just don't know. What if something happens
while we are gone?"

"Mom. I'm awake. The docs all say I look fine.
Go. Enjoy a nice dinner with Dad." And give me
a break from all the mom stuff. I don't say that out
loud, but I sure think it. I love my mom more than
anything, but she has exhausted me since I woke
up from my nap. She constantly fluffs my pillow
or gives me water. I need a break from her, but I
would never tell her that.

"Okay." Mom takes her purse from Dad but
turns back to me again. "Are you sure?"

"Yes, Mom. I'm sure. Go." I give her a classic
Max Greenwood smile to reassure her. The pain
meds must work pretty well for me because moving my head isn't aching as bad as it was.

Mom leans over the rail and kisses my forehead,

pushing back the hair from it like she has done a dozen times today. She doesn't say anything more until she gets to the door, when she stops and looks back at me.

"I'll make sure the nurses station has our numbers. I love you, Max."

"Love you too, Mom."

There are whispered voices as Mom and Dad leave the hospital room. I don't pay any attention to them. It's probably a nurse passing by or something. I hear the door click as it closes and I rest my eyes. Finally, a minute alone. But, I'm not alone. The hair on the back of my neck stands up like it does every time Tiba is near me. I feel her. My eyes pop open to see her just a few feet away from me at the foot of the bed.

"What are you doing here?" The sarcasm in my voice can't be missed.

"Um, your parents asked me to sit with you until they return." Tiba walks around the side of the bed closer to me.

"Well, you don't have to. I'm fine. You can leave now." I turn my head away from her and focus on the picture on the wall opposite where she stands. It's a big ugly flower. I put all my thoughts into that hideous picture, so I won't think about the woman on the other side of this stupid hospital bed.

"Not leaving. I told them I would stay, and I will. Besides, I need to talk to you."

"I've got nothing to say to you and don't want to hear anything you have to say." My voice says the words that my head tells it to, but my heart doesn't mean. I think I'll continue to listen to my head. My heart can't take being crushed again.

"I'm going to tell you anyway. I know you don't want to listen, but I beg you to. You don't have to respond, just listen. You don't even have to look at me if you don't want to."

Without moving, I don't respond. My focus remains on the picture, but I listen. I listen without breathing to see what she has to say. My heart rate increases even though I will it to slow down. Why does Tiba get to me this way? Why can't I just shut her out? But, I don't shut her out. I lay in this bed and wait. I wait for the words I want to hear, but don't want to hear. Tiba sighs behind me when she gets no response from me.

"Okay, then. I'm not going to make this a long story. You know my history. Gemma told you all about that. I will start with the night I left your house. When you told me about the problems at the job site, I just knew that my ex-husband had something to do with it. And yes, I said ex because that's what he is. Daniel took care of that for me and I'm officially divorced. And now I know that my ex had nothing to do with the problems at the job. But, you have to think about it from my perspective. I was scared. I've been scared for years. You're the first man that I've even given more than a date or two. You're the first man I have given my heart. I love you, Max. I left that day because I love you. I thought if I ran from you, you wouldn't be hurt. I was wrong to run. I know that now, but I didn't then."

Tiba pauses and takes a deep breath behind me. Her words repeat in my mind, but I can't get past the fact that she kept so much from me. I'm not even as upset about her running away, I can almost understand that part. What I can't fathom is how could she love me and not tell me any of the truth about herself. As if she can read my mind, Tiba continues.

"I know you're upset that I didn't tell you about my past. You have to understand that I've never told anyone but Gemma. It wasn't that I didn't want you to know, it's more of a survival technique for me. I thought if I kept it to myself, it would never come back to haunt me. I was wrong. I've been wrong about a lot of things. I spent a lot of time with a therapist while I was in Chicago. That's the reason I didn't come back sooner. I discovered that I needed to work on me before I could be the person you need me to be. I did that. I did that work. I have even followed up with the therapist since I've been here at the hospital. I talk to her twice a week by phone. I want to be that person, Max. I want to be the best person I can be." Tiba pauses again but only for a moment this time. "I love you, Max. I hope you can find it in yourself to forgive me for leaving, for not talking to you, for not being the person you thought I was. I hope you can get past that and give me another chance. But, if you can't, I'll understand. It's a lot for anyone to forgive. The one thing I want you to know is that I *do* love you. And that's not going to change no matter what you decide."

The flower picture on the wall has reds and oranges in it. It's bright and ugly. I would never put it in my house. I focus on those thoughts instead of the words that bounce around in my head. Tiba's words. *I love you, Max.* Over and over, her voice on repeat. Focus, Max. Deep green stems on the flower. The thing is huge. Why can't I keep my mind on this outrageous decoration? *Because you love her.* Stop! Don't think that.

I roll onto my back, still without looking at her. I don't say anything to her. I just lay in the hospital bed while dozens of things run through my head. Tiba's words, my injuries, the recovery period that I was told about earlier, holding Tiba, forgiving Tiba. So much I can't process it all at one time.

She moves to the side of the room and sits in one of the chairs. I cut my eyes to the side to see her as she watches me. I jerk my eyes back to the ceiling of the room. I don't want her to see me look at her. I don't know what to do, so I do nothing. The quiet in the room roars in my ears. How can it be this quiet in one place? I think I can hear my heart beating and it's not because there is a machine hooked up to it.

The quiet becomes more than I can bear. It feels like a weight bearing down on my body. I turn my head toward Tiba and her eyes lock with mine. The fist in my chest clinches again with power so hard I think I might pass out. I don't give in to it though. My head has to lead me right now.

"I don't know if I will ever forgive you. And I can't deal with any of it right now. I have to focus on my recovery."

Tiba's eyes mist over with unshed tears before she drops her head. I watch her shoulders slump and her hands entwine with each other. I feel the pain radiate from her and it hurts me. It physically hurts me to watch her, but I don't turn away. I want her to know I'm serious. After a moment, she raises her head and sits up straighter. She looks directly in my eyes and I see the pain she feels in her gaze.

"I understand."

Two simple words. She doesn't argue. She doesn't have to. I can see the words she doesn't say shine in her eyes. Disappointment, sadness, it all shows in those beautiful eyes. I hate to be the one to put those feelings there, but I am. I am that man. I honestly don't know if I can forgive her. My heart says I already have. But, I'm not listening to that part of my body. My brain says to stay far away. With so many conflicting emotions flowing through me, I don't have a choice but to push her away. I need all of my energy to recover.

Pulling my gaze from Tiba, I look back to the ceiling. I count the ceiling tiles to get my mind off of her. She doesn't move. She remains as still as a mannequin in that chair. I can feel her gaze on me, but I don't acknowledge it.

We remain like this for minutes that turn into hours. I count those stupid ceiling tiles over and over. Nurses come and go, aides come and go, but Tiba remains quietly on the other side of the room. I don't ask her to leave because I know she won't. She told my parents she would stay, and she will.

After what seems like a lifetime, I hear my parents' laughter as they enter the hospital room and it's an amazing sound. If nothing else, this night was good for them. The tension in the room stops them in their tracks. They both quieten and look from me to Tiba. Mom drops her purse on the nearest chair and slowly walks over to my bedside. Her eyes hold questions that I'm not ready to answer.

"You okay, son?"

"Yeah, Mom. I'm fine."

Mom glances from me to Tiba and back. Tiba stands and hugs my father before she walks to my beside to hug my mother.

"Hope you guys had a great time tonight. I'm going to go now." Tiba leaves the room before either of my parents can respond. Dad watches her walk out the door before he turns back to me.

"What happened here while we were gone?"

"Nothing I want to talk about, Dad."

Mom messes with the blanket on the bed before I grab her hand to stop her. "Stop, Mom. Just stop, okay." My voice is harsher than I mean it to be. Mom backs away from the bed with tears in her eyes.

"I'm sorry, Mom. I didn't mean that. I just mean that you don't have to fuss over me. Look, it's been a long day and I'm tired. I just want to go to sleep and get ready for therapy tomorrow, okay?" I reach my hand out toward my mother to show my regret in my previous words. She grabs it without hesitation. That's my mom, always there for me.

"It's okay, Max. You just woke up from a coma and have been hit from all sides with things. You rest now. I'll be here. Dad's going to go back to the hotel for the night."

"That's good. Dad, go get some rest. You look like you need it." I squeeze Mom's hand. "You do too, Mom. Why don't you go with him?"

My mother looks at me like I have grown two heads.

"I will not leave you here alone tonight. Now hush about that. Dad and I will take turns until we get you home."

Mom lets go of my hand and walks over to Dad. She gives him a kiss on the cheek and he pulls her into him in a hug. I turn my head to give them a moment. They whisper to each other, but I can't make out the words. Not sure I would want to if I could. I'm fortunate to have parents that still love each other as much as mine do. When they part, Dad walks to the side of the bed and takes my hand and squeezes it.

"Hope you can sleep in here tonight, son. You have a big day tomorrow. I love you." With that, Dad turns, pats my mom on the behind, which I did not need to see, and leaves the room. Mom pulls a chair up and props herself on the side of the bed with her arm.

"So, tell me what happened between you and Tiba."

"I told you I don't want to talk about it, Mom."

"I know, but that girl loves you and I know you love her. You two need to get past your differences and sort this out." Nothing like relationship advice from your mother.

"Mom, I can't even think about that right now. Tomorrow I start physical therapy to even be able to walk. I'm not the man Tiba thinks she loves. I am a shell of that man, in body and in mind. Until I can get back to the old me, I can't even think about anything else. And, I'm not sure I can forgive her anyway." I turn my head away from Mom. I don't want to see the disappointment in her eyes.

"You can, son. You just have to let yourself forgive her. That's what love is all about. We all make mistakes." Mom reaches out and takes my hand in hers. "Just think about it. But you are right, your focus does need to be on healing, so I'll drop it for now."

I hear the scratch of the chair on the floor as Mom scoots it backwards. She lets go of my hand and pulls my damn blanket up again. I cut my eyes to her and she laughs. She actually laughs at me. She throws both hands in the air and backs away from the bed.

"Sorry! I forgot. It's a mom thing."

A smile works its way to my lips and I can't help but let it out. Mom returns the smile and plops into a chair. She picks up a book off of the small table next to the chair and opens it to a page she had marked.

"Go to sleep, son. Rest up for tomorrow. I love you."

"I love you too, Mom."

With that, I close my eyes and think about the day. I wake up from a coma to find out that I've been out for almost three weeks. I find out that two of my own workers attacked me and were the same ones that were vandalizing the job site. That was quite a shock. It just shows that people can be bought since they both admitted to being paid by one of the firms that lost the bid to us.

After digesting all of that, I find out that I had a brain injury, a new hip, and rods in my leg. And, I have to do intense physical therapy to be able to walk much less run on that leg. Then, to top it all off, Tiba begs my forgiveness and tells me she loves me. That's the part that my mind keeps going back to. Not the injuries, not the job, just Tiba. As much as I want to tell her that I love her too, I can't do it. I can't open myself up like that, especially now.

What if I did tell her and then she realized that she loved the old Max, not the newly injured, recovering Max? Nope, I can't do that. I will not set myself up for that heartbreak again. She broke me once, but she won't break me again. I'm too broken from everything else right now.

Chapter 22

TIBA

THE DING OF THE SHOP door opening draws my eyes to it. Charley runs into the salon with Gemma behind her. I smile from ear to ear when I see them. After a long day behind the chair, the sight of these two is just what I need.

"Auntie T!" Charley squeals as she runs into my open arms.

"Hey, sweetheart. I've sure missed you." I feel Charley's tiny arms squeeze my neck as we hug. I close my eyes and revel in that feeling.

"I've missed you, too! Where have you been?"

Charley's innocent question brings me back to the last few months. From being in Chicago to being at the hospital until Max was released. Max isn't the only person I disappeared from. When I ran, I left everyone I care about behind.

"I had some things I had to do." I stand, picking Charley up and putting her in my salon chair. "But, all that's done now and I'm back."

"You left without saying goodbye." Charley pushes her bottom lip out in a pout. Her words drive a stake through my heart, showing me just how selfish my running away was. I put my hands on the arms of the chair and squat to where we are eye level.

"I'm so sorry, Charley. I promise you I won't ever do that to you again." I hold my breath before I ask the next question since I haven't had great luck with it lately. "Will you forgive me?"

Charley reaches out and hugs me again. "Of course, Auntie T. I love you!"

I let out the breath I was holding with relief. I grab her and pick her up in a tight grip.

"I love you too, Charley. More than you'll ever know."

Out of the corner of my eye, I see Gemma with tears in her eyes. I put Charley down to the floor and hand her a comb from my station. She takes it and runs over to Gemma's station where she has a doll that she always "works on" when she comes to the salon. I grab a tissue from the counter and pass it to Gemma. She quickly wipes the tears away and gives me a hug.

"Sorry. I'm so emotional lately. I don't know why." She backs away and plops into the chair at my station. "I guess I'm just tired from all that with Max. Now that he's home, maybe we all can get some rest."

"Yeah, I guess maybe we can." I turn away from Gemma and fiddle with things on my counter, straightening things that don't need to be straightened. I feel Gemma's hand on my arm. I stop, but don't turn around.

"Have you heard from him?"

"No." I still don't turn around. Tears form in my eyes. How many days will I cry over this man?

"Give him time. He'll come around. Kathleen

says he has a very intense therapy schedule and is pushing himself really hard right now." Gemma drops her hand and leans back in the chair. I look at the ceiling willing the tears to stop. After brushing them away, I turn back to face her.

"I don't think I'll hear from him. As much as I wish it, I don't think it will happen. But that's okay. I told him how I feel, and I can't force him to feel the same way." Damn tears, back again.

"Oh, Tiba. I'm so sorry. I don't know what to do to make it better for either of you." Gemma looks so distraught as she twists her hands.

"Gem, there's nothing you can do. And nothing you *need* to do. Max and I had a few great days together and I messed it up. Now, we move on. Max works on his recovery and I go back to doing what I have always done, surviving. And thanks to you, Raef, and Daniel, I can do that without fear now. I have nothing hanging over my head any more. I am finally free to live." I manage a small smile. It's a good feeling to know I'm free, even if my heart is broken over Max.

"I just want you to be happy. I want you to have what I have with Raef."

"I will one day, girlie. I believe that. Right now, I have all that I need. I have you and Raef. I have that beautiful little girl over there that I couldn't love any more if she was my own child. I have Jack and Kathleen, both of which contact me regularly to check on me. You guys are all my family. That's all I need." My smile is more genuine this time. I do have all that I *need*. Max is what I want. As much as my heart hurts, I know I can make it without him, that I *have* to make it without him. I can still want him, love him. I just can't have him.

"I know you're right. It just hurts me to see my two best friends hurt. And to know that it is so easy to fix that hurt. If only Max wasn't so damned stubborn."

"Ohhh, Mommy! You said a bad word!" Charley calls out from across the room with a reminder that little ears hear everything. Gemma and I look at each other and burst into laughter. Once we start, we can't seem to stop, to the point Charley comes over to check on us.

"What's wrong? Why you laughing?" Charley asks with her nose scrunched in confusion. This seems to make us laugh even more. Tears roll down both our cheeks and I double over holding my stomach.

"We're fine, Charley," I manage to squeeze out as I catch my breath.

"Grown-ups are weird." Charley turns and goes back across the room to her doll. Her statement sets us off again and Charley just looks at us and shakes her little head. We have been schooled by a four-year old.

"Oh, my goodness, I needed that."

"Me too, Gem. Me too." We are both breathless as we try to regain our composure. "And when did Charley grow up so much? She sounded like a teenager just then."

"Girl, you don't know the half of it. These last few weeks, Raef and I have felt like we have teen or pre-teen. Attitude! I love it though. She's so sassy." Gemma whispers to me so Charley doesn't over hear. "Raef loves her sassiness too, even though he won't admit it."

"My daddy says I'm like Auntie Marie." Charley again lets us know she hears us. Gemma and I can't help but giggle.

"Lordy, girlie. You are going to have your hands full!" I grab Gemma's hand and pull her out of the chair. "How about I take you girls out for pizza?"

"Can we, Mommy? Can we?" Charley drops her doll and the comb and runs across the salon.

"Absolutely!" Gemma takes Charley's much smaller hand in hers. "I think a girls' night out is just what we all need."

"I think so too! Just let me run in the back and get my purse."

"Go ahead. Charley needs to clean up her mess over at *her* station." Gemma gently turns Charley toward where she just dropped everything.

"Ugh, Mommy." Charley pokes out that lip and droops over with her arms hanging in front of her. "Do I have to?"

"Yes, ma'am. You do" Charley stalks away as Gemma covers her mouth to keep her laughter at bay. I shake my head and hold my chuckle in until I reach the office area.

A quick look around tells me that everything is in order for me to leave. I grab my purse from the desk drawer. For the first time in a long time, I'm actually excited to do something. Nothing like a good night out with your best friend and niece. Things are looking up.

Chapter 23

MAX

"**D**AMN, COLLEEN. YOU'VE PUT ME through the ringer today." My physical therapy assistant laughs at me while I sit up from the therapy mat. Every day the exercises get a little tougher, but I'm determined to walk without this stupid cane as soon as possible. I've moved to it from the walker they had me on when I left the hospital. I'm tired of feeling like an old man.

"You asked for it, Max. But, you're ready to push harder. You're already way ahead of where most patients with your injuries are." Colleen gives me a smile over the folder where she makes notes from my session.

My therapist is a beautiful girl, blonde hair and blue eyes, everything I used to go for. There was a day that I would be very attracted to her, but these days the only woman on my mind is Tiba. Even though I spend three days a week with Colleen during therapy, I haven't had one moment where I felt like I wanted her. As I watch her finish up her notes, I think about how much my life has changed in the last few months.

Tiba and I had a whirlwind of a few days that

led to what can only be described as heartbreak. From there I went back into survival mode, albeit a much different one than when Gemma and Raef married. I dove into my work, living and breathing Greenwood Construction. That is, until the incident that brought me here to therapy. The attack at the job left me a broken man. Tiba left me broken emotionally and work left me broken physically.

Now, I'm trying to put myself back together. I've been out of the hospital for two weeks and have thrown myself into therapy. As my body heals, my heart is also healing. I've spent hours going over in my mind the things Tiba said to me in my hospital room. I believe now that she does love me. I believe that she regrets how she handled things and I am slowly coming to the realization that I have forgiven her. Not only for leaving me, but for not being honest with me from the beginning. She did the only thing she knew how to do. That was her survival mode.

My problem is that I don't know where to go from here. I've made such an ass of myself to Tiba that I don't know how to repair the damage I've done. Gemma assures me that it would only take a conversation to turn things around, but I'm not so sure. Then there is the issue of my injuries. I am still not the man I was before the attack and I don't want to be a man that Tiba has to take care of. I want to fix things and take care of her. I suppose I just need more time to figure it all out.

"Hey, Max. Come back to earth." Colleen's voice brings me back to the present. I'm embarrassed that she caught me deep in my thoughts, a place I find myself too much these days.

"Sorry. Just thinking." My cheeks feel warm. What the hell, am I blushing? I duck my head so Colleen doesn't notice. I certainly don't want my therapist to think I'm a silly teenager trapped in a man's body.

"Not a problem." Colleen chuckles as she opens the therapy room door and extends the folder my direction. "You know the drill, take the folder to the receptionist and I'll see you in a couple of days. You're making great progress but keep using that cane. Don't try to get too far ahead of yourself by doing too much too soon."

Colleen leaves the room when I take the folder from her. I look at the cane in my hand. I hate this thing, but it does help me since my balance has been off after getting back on my feet. The docs tell me it's nothing to worry about and will all settle back to normal soon. My right hip and leg just went through quite a lot and my body has to get used to my weight back on that side.

Stopping by the reception desk, I pay for the session and make sure my next appointment is set. I'm ready to get out of here. Gemma is supposed to be the one here to take me home today. Dad dropped me off, but he had to get back to the job site. Unfortunately, it will still be awhile until I can drive since it is my right side that is injured. The doc won't even consider releasing me to do that for at least another two weeks, maybe more.

When I push through the door into the waiting room, I scan the area for Gemma. I don't find her. Instead, I see a head of crazy curly hair turned downward focused on a magazine. Tiba. My breath catches at the sight of her and I stop before I am fully through the door. My God, she's gorgeous. I haven't seen her since that day in my hospital room. My parents told me she stayed in the waiting room until I was released a few days later, but she never came back to my room.

As if she senses me watching her, Tiba raises her gaze from the magazine and locks with mine. She slowly stands, drops the magazine on the table, and makes her way toward me. I don't move until a nurse comes to call the next patient, forcing me to step away from the door and toward Tiba. By this time, she stands directly in front of me. My nerve endings tingle all over my body being this close to her.

"Hey, big guy. You ready to break out of this joint?" She reaches out and touches my arm. The tingles where she touches me become more like electrical shocks. I do believe the hair on my arms is standing up.

"Um, yeah. Sure." I stutter through my words. "Where's Gemma?"

"She called and asked for me to pick you up. She isn't feeling well again. Raef finally talked her into going to the doctor, so she's headed there."

Tiba gently encourages me forward with her hand still on my arm. Her touch makes each step I take even more unsteady than normal. She notices as I take a small stumble. Her hand grips tighter around my arm and she steps closer to me.

"Do you need me to help?"

"No! I don't need help!" I jerk my arm away from her grasp. The loss of her touch saddens me, but I will not tolerate pity from anyone, not even her.

She jumps away from me and all eyes in the waiting room turn to us. They watch as Tiba nods and moves ahead of me to hold the outside door open for me. I tuck my head in embarrassment of my outburst, then steady myself and move past her through the door.

"I'm sorry," I mutter as I pass her.

She doesn't respond, simply walks on past me to her car. She opens the door to the passenger side and leaves it open. She doesn't wait for me to catch up, just gets in the driver's seat and starts the car. My slow pace finally gets me there and I ease down into the seat. After I maneuver my lovely cane inside with us, I close the door and Tiba wastes no time putting the car in drive and pulling out of the parking space.

Not able to take the silence from her any longer, I reach over and grab her hand from the steering wheel when she stops at the road coming out of the lot. She doesn't turn to look at me, but she doesn't pull her hand back.

"I'm really sorry about that back there." The subdued, regretful tone of my voice must get to her because she finally turns her head and levels me with those big brown eyes. They let me know she isn't totally convinced of my apology. "Look, I'm having a lot of trouble dealing with being an invalid. When you asked to help, I took it the wrong way. I don't want pity from anyone. I just want to be independent like I've always been. I'm really sorry I snapped at you."

Her eyes gloss over as she stares at me. The realization of what I tried to impress upon her sinks in. She recognizes that I just want to be the old Max, not this person I am right now. She squeezes my hand before she pulls hers from mine, focuses back on the road, and pulls out of the parking lot.

"You're not an invalid. You can get around with caney boy over there. And I don't pity you. I'm proud of how far you've come."

A smile sprouts from the corners of my mouth. "*Caney boy*? You're naming my cane now?" My smile turns into laughter and I can't help but throw my head back in a full belly laugh. This is the first time I've laughed since Tiba left. It sure does feel good. I look over at her and she grins silently as she drives.

"Only you would name my cane. And only you can make me laugh about it." I reach out and place my hand on her leg. She jumps when I do and her head jerks from the road to me. "Watch the road, driver."

Tiba turns her eyes back to the road but not before I see the questions there. She wants to know what I'm doing touching her like this. Hell, I want to know too. This isn't how I planned to approach her and certainly not when I planned to. Something about being around her again after so long just makes me not want to wait. I want to tell her how I feel, and I want to tell her now. Of course, in a car isn't the right way to do that. I'll wait until we get to my house.

What if she doesn't want me like this? The thought grabs me by the throat and constricts my breath. I can't think about that. If it happens, I'll have to deal with it, but I can't think about it now. I've discussed this with my father many times over the last couple of weeks and he tells me over and over to not think about what might happen, only about what I know I can control. And that is letting Tiba know how I feel about her.

We drive the rest of the way to my house making small talk. I keep the conversation going by prompting her to talk about what she's been doing since I've been out of the hospital. She tells me about work and how it's great to be back doing what she loves. I tell her about therapy and what a pain, literally, it has been. Before I know it, we are at the house. She puts the car in park but makes no move to get out.

"You want to come in for a little bit? I could use a steady hand going up the steps."

Tiba hesitates for a moment, then nods. I exhale the breath I was holding, open the car door, and wrestle caney boy out of the car. She watches me until I get my right leg out of the vehicle before she opens her door and gets out. Before I can completely stand, she has rounded the car and waits for me.

She closes the car door behind me and we both walk the few steps that lead to my porch. I grab the step-rail with one hand, the other on my cane. She doesn't touch me, waiting for me to guide her in what I want.

"Just put your hand on my back while I go up. It helps steady me."

Tiba does as I ask, and I feel her tiny fingers through my shirt. I don't move, just stand and enjoy her touch. Finally, I take a deep breath and make the first step. Steps and stairs still bother my leg, another thing I am told will just take time. We slowly work our way to the top, with me moving both feet to each step. No running up them for me anymore.

"Whew! I hate those things these days." I dig in my pocket for the house key. When I find it, I pass it to Tiba and let her open the door. She moves her hand from my back and I wish I would have just kept the key, so she would have kept her hand on me.

"Does it hurt?" She tilts her head toward my leg.

"Sometimes. On steps mostly, but it aches sometimes too." We both get through the door and I drop into one of the chairs in my living room. I stretch my bad leg out in front of me and put it on the ottoman I keep close to this chair since I've been home from the hospital. "My therapist says I am trying to do too much too fast. I just want to get back to normal."

"You don't want to overdo and have a setback."

"You sound like my therapist and doctor." I chuckle. Tiba is still standing so I motion to the other chair and couch. "Will you stay for a little bit and visit with me?"

She casts me an uncertain look but she moves around my chair and sits across from me on the couch. I watch as she looks around the living room. Even though she has been here before, she looks at it like it's the first time. Her gaze roams around the room, pausing on the massive fireplace, until it lands back on me. She blushes when she finds me watching her.

"Sorry, you just have such a beautiful home." Tiba tucks her head slightly as she pushes her hair away from her face.

"Thanks. I love it. It's my place to relax and

unwind." She nods but doesn't say anything. With a deep breath, I decide that now is the time for me to move forward. "But, the house isn't why I wanted you to come in. I want to talk to you about something."

Tiba turns and meets my eyes. The frown on her face tells me that she's concerned about this conversation. Her eyes don't leave mine even though they are full of uncertainty. I move my leg off the ottoman and slide over directly in front of her. She flinches when I take both of her hands in mine, not sure what to think of my forward move. She doesn't pull them back, though, so I take that as a good sign and continue.

"Tiba, when you came to me in the hospital, I didn't react very well. I look back and am ashamed of how I treated you. I'm not trying to make excuses, but I was overwhelmed that day. After just waking up and finding out I had been attacked at work, then you telling me you love me. My brain was still fuzzy, and I didn't know what to do. It took me a few days to realize that I handled it all wrong with you and for that I'm sorry." I pause as I look into her eyes for an indication of how she feels. I see a flash of what I would like to think is acceptance of my apology, but it's quickly replaced by the pervious uncertainty. I want to replace that look as quickly as possible.

"I love you, Tiba. That's why I was so upset when you left and when I found out everything else. I love you. Heart and soul. Every bit of me." I pause again, weighing her reaction. A single tear escapes her eye. I wipe it away with my thumb, my palm lingers on her cheek. "You asked that day if I could forgive you. There's nothing to forgive. You did what you felt you had to do to survive. I understand that now. After everything that I've done to push you away, I'm in front of you hoping *you* can forgive me."

Tiba eyes me for a moment, then leans her face against my hand. That gentle movement as she closes her eyes gives me hope. Hope that I haven't had in a long time.

When she opens her eyes, both are filled with tears. She takes my hand in hers and pulls it from her cheek to her lips. She kisses my palm ever so gently, so softly that I wonder if I imagined it. She eases our connected hands to her lap. I wait for her to speak. Her silence concerns me to the point I fidget on the ottoman, moving closer to her.

She drops her face toward the floor for a moment before she looks back to me, eye to eye. The golden flecks shine in the dark brown as tears stream down her face. And still I wait. Finally, after I feel like I've lived five lifetimes, a small smile breaks on her lips.

"I forgive you, Max. I gave you every reason to push me away. How could I ever hold that against you?"

Relief floods through my veins. I reach for Tiba with my free hand, squeezing and pulling her other hand toward me at the same time. She slides off the couch onto the ottoman with me. I move back a little to give her room, not like she needs much for her tiny body.

"Oh, thank goodness! You had me worried when you were so quiet!" I hold her tight against my body. "I know I'm not the man I was before, but I'm on the mend. Will you take a broken man like me and give me a second chance?"

"Max! You aren't broken!" She pulls away and places one hand on each side of my face, holding my gaze with hers. "You are perfect, injured or not. You are perfect for me." With that, she leans in and kisses me.

What a feeling, Tiba's soft lips on mine. Such a soft sweet kiss, but it stirs something inside me that's been dormant since she left. Desire. I haven't felt any desire for anyone since Tiba. I had begun to think I would never feel that way again. In one kiss, it suddenly roars its way back to life.

Moving one hand to the back of her head, I tilt it and pull her tighter against my lips. I touch her lips with a quick swipe of my tongue and she opens to me fully. The sweet kiss ignites into one filled with passion. All of the loneliness of the last few months flies away in that kiss. Eventually, I pull back as we both pant to catch our breath. Her eyes glow with desire, the gold flecks prominent. I slide my arm around her and pull her body back against mine, her head tucked against my neck, my chin rests lightly above.

"I love you, Tiba. And God knows, I've missed you." I sigh as I close my eyes, holding her close.

"I love you, too, Max. I've loved you for so long." Tiba's arms snake their way around my middle as she holds me as tightly as I hold her. It's as if we both feel the other might disappear any second. "I think I've loved you since the first time you walked into the salon. I just kept it to myself because Gemma is my best friend. And, well, you know the rest of that."

"I wish I had known back then. Maybe it

would've knocked some since into me sooner."

"I don't know. I think everything happens for a reason."

"You're probably right. It certainly helps me know that what I feel for you is so much more than anything I've ever felt."

"Me too, big guy, me too."

"Tiba, I've got a long way to go with my recovery and I know this is sudden, but I don't want to lose you again." I pull my head back far enough to where I can look her in the eye. "If we do this, I'm in it for the long haul. I'm not saying we rush off and get married, but I'm saying that someday I want the whole shebang, marriage, family, white picket fence. All of it. I'm all in."

She stiffens in my arms. Her eyes dart away from mine. Have I said too much too soon? I've never been one for delayed gratification. If I want something, I go for it. And I want a life with Tiba. Everyone may think I'm crazy for moving so quickly, but I don't know that I'll survive if I lose her again.

"Did I say something wrong?" Fear grips me as she eases her way out of my arms and moves back to the couch. She raises her eyes back to mine and I see sadness in them. Her lips are downturned, and her forehead is scrunched in an anxious frown.

"Max, before we can move forward, or if we can move forward, I need to tell you something."

If. That's the only word I hear. It can't be if. I won't let her go. Whatever she has to tell me, I won't let her go.

"You can tell me anything, Tiba." I reach out to grab her hands, but she pulls them closer to her body, twisting them almost in the same manner Gemma does when she is anxious.

"You know about Gerard, my ex. And how he beat me and I almost died." She watches as I nod. "Well, there was damage to my body that I've never shared with anyone other than my parents. And you know I don't talk to them."

"I'm so sorry that happened to you. If he wasn't in prison, I would kill him for what he did to you." My hands grip into fists as I get angry all over again when I think about him hurting Tiba.

"Max, you need to listen to me. What he did to me left me with one permanent problem." Tiba drops her gaze to the floor. "I can't have children. I can't give you everything you just said you want."

My fists clinch tighter. Not in anger at her, but anger toward the man that did this to her, that took this away from her. I will never get to see a little Tiba or Max running around the yard. The realization hits me hard, but I quickly know that it doesn't matter. As long as I have her, I have what I need. I just have to convince her of that.

"Tiba, look at me." I angle her face toward me with my hand under her chin. My knuckles slide up the side of her cheek, taking her tears with my hand. "It's okay, baby. I'm sorry I said all that before. I didn't know. If you can't have children, then it'll just be you and me."

"But you want kids, Max. You just said so!" Tiba jumps from the couch in despair.

"It's honestly not something I ever spent a lot of time thinking about. I just kind of assumed it would happen because that's what usually happens with couples." I ease up to a standing position. My

leg has stiffened, and it takes me a minute to get to
Tiba. Once I do, I pull her to me. "Baby, as long as
I have you, that's all I need. We'll build our future
together and if we decide later that we want kids,
there are many ways we can fulfill that."

Her tears soak through my shirt. It breaks my
heart for her to hurt like this. I ease her with me
to the couch and pull her down onto my lap. Pain
radiates through my leg as we land. I inhale sharply
and she notices. She tries to move away from me,
but I hold her in place.

"*Shhh*, baby. It's okay. Just not used to sitting
down so quickly. Please stay here."

My arms tighten around her and she leans into
my chest. We remain like that for several minutes
before I break the silence.

"You've never told anyone about this?" It shocks
me that she never told Gemma.

"Only my parents when they came to the hospital after it all happened. They were there when
I had surgery, a hysterectomy. So, you see, there is
absolutely no way around this with me. I can't have
children." Tiba's tears flood again. It's apparent that
she has never really dealt with this and it's all coming out with her tears now.

"Baby, it's really okay. You are perfect. Remember
what you just told me. It's the same for me with
you. You are perfect for me."

"But you can be fixed, and I can't."

"I know you won't think it compares, but the
doctors aren't sure that I won't have a limp, possi-
bly for the rest of my life. Are you okay being with
me with a limp?"

"Of course! I don't care if you limp or even if

you can't walk at all! I love you!" she exclaims as she sits up straight in my lap.

"Well, that's how I feel about you. I don't care if you can't have children, Tiba. I love you! I love all of you, just like you are. Okay." I kiss her gently. "I. Love. You."

She slumps against me. My arms are wrapped around her and her hand rests next to her face on my chest. Her fingers move lightly as she fidgets. It's almost like her fingers replicate the thoughts going on in her mind.

"Okay," Tiba whispers against my body. So softly I'm not sure she really said it out loud.

"Okay?"

"Okay. I'm all in, too." Her fingers tighten against my shirt pulling it into her palm in a ball.

"Oh, baby! I'm so happy you said that." I slide her up to where our faces are aligned. "We will make this work. All of it."

Her arm slips around my neck and her hand snakes into my hair, while her other hand remains firmly attached to my shirt. I slide one hand up her back and press her into me and kiss her with all of the love I have inside me. This woman is willing to take a chance on me after everything and I want her to know just how much that means to me.

No matter what faces us, Tiba is my everything and I'm going to make sure she has nothing but happiness in the future. She has been through so much and I added to that by pushing her away. I have so much to make up for and it starts right now.

Chapter 24

TIBA

MAX'S HANDS ROAM BY BACK. One has slipped under my shirt and lightly touches my skin. Oh, how I've missed his touch. We kiss and kiss on the couch until he pulls back and levels me with his eyes. They are so very green with desire. He opens his mouth to say something but closes it just as quickly.

"Say it, Max. Whatever it is you want to say, just say it."

"I want you, Tiba. I know this is all being thrown at you today, but I want you." His brow furrows in despair.

"I can feel that, big guy." I squirm against his lap and chuckle. "I want you too. It's not too fast. It's just right. It all feels right."

Max kisses me again and presses me down against his erection. It stops my squirming and a moan escapes my mouth. Just as quickly as he kisses me, he stops. He drops his forehead to mine, his breath heavy.

"Let's move this to the bedroom. I don't think this couch will work well with my leg."

"Oh, Max! I didn't even think about that. Maybe

we shouldn't do this now. You need to heal." I jump from the couch and wonder if I've hurt him.

"Tiba, as long as you are willing, we are doing this." Max eases off the couch and takes my hand. "Just hand me caney boy over there and let's get to the bedroom. It'll be like you're with an old man."

I grab Max's cane and pass it to him. I can't help but laugh at his joke about being an old man. He is far from that. Even with being down for weeks, his body is still rock hard, nothing about it old.

Once in the bedroom, he leans his cane against the bedside table and turns to me. His hands glide up my sides, taking my shirt with them. I raise my arms to let him remove it. As soon as mine is gone, I make quick work of his. My hands travel across his chest in wonder at how fit he is. My fingers move across the ripples of his muscles until they rest on his hips.

"After all you've been through, how in the world are you in such great shape?"

"Weights. I've lifted with my upper body since I got out of the hospital."

"Hmmm. Well I'm glad to be the benefactor of that. You are pretty smoking hot!"

Max pauses after he slips my skirt from my hips and lets it drop to the floor. A frown crosses his face. He takes one hand and rubs it across his jaw.

"You won't think that when you see the scars from my surgeries." Max tries to turn away from me. With my hands still on his hips, I stop him and keep him in front of me.

"Max. Give me your hand." He puts his hand in my outstretched one and I move it to my lower abdomen. "Feel those spots? Those are my scars.

Our scars don't define us."

He continues to run his hand across my skin even after I drop mine. He eases down to where his face is flush with my stomach, even though a flash of pain crosses his face. His lips replace his fingers as he kisses each of my scars. My dark skin hides them well, but they are most definitely there. Right now, with Max's kisses tingling over each one, I am even more appreciative of the scars. They mean I survived. I survived and found what love is supposed to be.

I shiver with excitement as he stands again. He pulls my bra down which pushes my breasts above it. His teeth scrape along my hardened nipple, eliciting a gasp from me. He chuckles against my skin and does the same thing to the other breast, his nip a little harder. Shocks run through my body from head to toe as my desire ratchets to levels I have only felt with Max.

He straightens back up and gazes at me. I am bare before him with the exception of a scrap of lace panties and my displaced bra. I blush at the intense look on his face. He reaches to remove the bra and then eases the panties down my legs to the where my skirt is pooled at my feet.

"You are so beautiful." Max's hands skim up my legs. My head falls back in pleasure when he reaches my center, his touch brings instant ecstasy.

My fingers grab the side of the jogging pants he wears and pull them down as far as I can while in his grasp. His hands leave my skin and replace mine on his pants. I hear a stark intake of breath from him before he drops his pants to the floor, followed by his underwear. He takes my hand in his and places it on the scar on his hip. My eyes follow my hand and see the red mark where our fingers touch.

"My doctor says my scars are *angry*. But he says they are perfectly normal and will look better over time." Max drops his hand to his side, but I gently rub my fingers along the line of the scar. He extends his leg toward me and points to the scars on it. "There are the other beauties."

Dropping to my knees, I ease my fingers along his skin, touching the scars as I go. My lips follow my fingers and I do as he did for me earlier. I place gentle kisses along each scar from tip to tip. I move back up his leg and do the same on the scar on his hip. His hands grasp my shoulders as he groans. It's a sound of desire mixed with pain. I immediately pull back and look up to his face.

"Did I hurt you?"

Max's hand slips from my shoulder to my cheek, his thumb gently rubs my face.

"No, baby. You didn't hurt me. When you kissed my scars, it was a bit overwhelming for me. I was scared I would never have you with me again, much less have you accept me like this." He brings me back to stand in front of him and kisses me. The kiss is full of more than just passion, it is full of emotion. It is full of love.

We ease down on the bed, side by side. As we kiss, our hands roam each other's bodies like it's our first time together, each touch full of desire. Max's large body and my much smaller one fit together like pieces of a puzzle. He is the piece of the puzzle of my life that was always missing.

His lips ease away from me and he rolls to his

back, pulling me on top of him as he does.

"You're going to have to take the lead tonight, baby." He holds me as I raise myself above him.

"I don't want to hurt you. I don't want my weight to hurt your hip." I hold myself over Max without putting my full weight on him. I feel his erection against me but don't move to take him in.

"Oh, baby. You won't hurt me. You don't weigh enough to hurt me. Besides, I won't be thinking of anything other than how you feel around me." He reaches between us and places his erection at my entrance. "I want you, Tiba. I *need* you. There's a condom in the night table."

"Well, you know I can't get pregnant and I haven't been with anyone but you in a very long time, so . . ."

"Since I've had every test in the world while in the hospital, I'm clean. And I haven't been with anyone since you. I haven't *wanted* anyone since you." Max groans as he rubs himself against me. "And I would very much love to feel you without any barriers."

He uses his free hand to encourage me to lower myself onto him. I slowly take him in, a process that takes some time due to his size, watching his face the entire time to see if I cause him any pain. He holds my gaze and I see nothing other than desire. Once my body accommodates him, I stop and rest gently against his hips, the fullness of him almost overwhelming.

"Are you okay?" My voice is breathless as I hold still against him.

"I'm more than okay. You feel amazing." Max grasps my own hips and moves me upward. "You need to move, baby. I need to feel you move."

He doesn't have to encourage me any more than that. Slowly, I begin move above him as his hands wander from my hips to my breasts, caressing them. My hands are on his hard chest, steadying me as I move.

"You are so sexy above me like this." His gaze wanders over my body.

The race to my orgasm begins more quickly than I expect, and my movements increase. Max's hands drop back to my hips and helps my motions. His brow furrows and he bites his lip.

"I'm not going to last much longer, baby," he grinds out between groans. My own moan escapes my lips.

"I'm right there with you." I tell him just as I feel the sensations of my orgasm hit me. I can feel myself grip him and I keep moving until his grasp tightens on my hips. Our bodies slam together as he raises his hips off the bed to meet me and he lets go.

"Tiba!" Max growls as he comes inside me. He holds me tight against him and his body shakes. After he is spent, he drops his hips back to the bed, taking my body with him. I fall against his chest and rest there while he holds me. "Wow, baby. That was . . . there are no words for what that was."

"I agree. No words." We are both still as we pant to catch our breath. When I come back to earth, I remember his hip injury. I pop up and off of him in one motion. "Your hip. Are you okay?"

Max chuckles as he turns on his side. He pulls me back down beside him in the bed. "My hip is fine. I may be a little sore after this, but that was the best thing that's happened to me in weeks." He pulls me back against his body and I feel him beginning to harden again. He grinds his hips toward me.

"No sir, big guy. No more of that today. We are not going to overdo until you're fully healed." I slip my hips backwards. He grabs me with one hand and pulls my hips back to him. He is almost fully erect again.

"But, somebody just got to play and he wants to play again." Max presses into me.

"Well, he isn't going to play like that." I hop off the bed and watch him over my shoulder as I walk to the bathroom. "But, after I clean you up, I may know of a way to take care of your little problem over there."

"Little problem? Nothing little about this, sweetheart!" He grabs his erection in his hand.

I throw back my head and laugh.

"You're right, *big guy*! Nothing little about you." I am still chuckling when I walk in the bathroom to grab a towel.

When I walk back into the bedroom, Max is sprawled out in all his provocative glory across the bed. He watches me as I casually sashay across the room. I take the view of his body in as I look at every glorious inch of him. Yes, I can take care of that problem he has going on and not hurt him. And he will enjoy it as much as I will.

Chapter 25

MAX

TIBA'S HEAD IS ON MY chest, her leg splayed across the top of mine. My arm is wrapped around her with my hand gently rubbing circles on her back. After we made love and I mentioned us doing it again, she shut me down quickly. She was too worried about my injuries. Instead, she wound up pleasuring me with her mouth. Now, I am exhausted and spent. I definitely will have to make that one up to her soon. I did not expect her to jump in and take care of me like that.

"What are you thinking right now?" Tiba's husky voice gets my attention.

"Well, if you want the truth, I was thinking about how good you just made me feel and how I need to return the favor very soon."

"No need to return the favor." She giggles against my chest. "But, I'll let you if you want to."

"Oh, I definitely want to. I'm obviously not in the shape I'm used to being in because I am zapped right now. Give me a little rest and I'm coming for you, baby."

"We can take a nap if you want to. Then I can either cook us dinner or run out and pick us up something."

"A nap sounds great. As long as you're next to me." I stop my caresses on Tiba's back and pull her tighter against me to emphasize my point. "And then, I'm going to take you out for dinner. A real date."

She smiles and her arm that hangs over my side grips me as she hugs me. "I like the sound of that." Her voice is almost a whisper.

"Good. Now let's get that nap."

My fingers begin to wander on her back again as I close my eyes. The feel of Tiba's body next to mine relaxes me more than anything has in weeks. It doesn't take but a few minutes until I feel her breaths even out and I know she has dozed off. I can tell I won't be far behind her.

Just as I fall asleep, my phone dings at almost the same time Tiba's does. It's the sound of a text message on my phone and I assume the same on hers. I reach over to the bedside table and ease my phone into my hand so as to not wake her. So far so good, she's still asleep.

When I open my messages, I see the incoming group one is from Gemma.

Will you come out to the farm in about an hour? Raef and I need to talk to you.

What a strange message. What in the world would Raef and Gemma need with me that requires us to all be at the farm? Unless . . . something's wrong. Maybe it's Charley. She didn't mention Charley. Surely if something had happened to her, Gemma would say that and not leave me hanging.

Sure. I'll be there. Is everyone okay?

Just be at the farm. We'll tell everyone at once.

Too cryptic for me. I wonder if Tiba's text was the same as mine. As much as I hate to wake her, if we are going to the farm, we need to get up. With one hand on her back, I ease her head back with my other hand. Once I can see her face, I lean in and kiss her. She stirs but doesn't waken. I kiss her again.

"Baby. You need to wake up." Gentle kisses all over her face finally bring her awake.

"Hey. How long have I been asleep?"

"Not long, but I got a strange message from Gemma. You had a message too. You may want to check your phone."

Tiba sits up in the bed with the covers pooled at her waist. Her breasts are right at my eye level since I have my head propped on my arm. They are very enticing, and it takes everything in me to keep my hands to myself. Instead, I watch her climb out of the bed in search of her phone. She finds it on the floor in a pile of our clothes.

"I have a message from Gemma, too." Tiba opens her message app. "It says for me to go out to your parents' farm in an hour. She said that she and Raef need to talk to me." She looks up from her phone, her eyes wide with concern.

"Same message I got." I sit up in the bed and lean back against the headboard. "I asked if everyone is okay and she just said that they wanted to tell everyone at once."

Tiba grabs her clothes off the floor and starts to get dressed. She shoots me a withering look when I don't jump out of bed to follow her.

"What are you waiting for? We need to go!" She grabs my shirt from the floor and throws it at me.

I catch it right before it hits me and drop it beside me while I ease myself over to the edge of the bed.

"Hey. Calm down. They said an hour." I pull her between my legs where I sit on the bedside. "It only takes 30 minutes to get there. And, I need a shower."

Tiba folds her body into me and drops her head to my shoulder, burrowing her neck into mine. I wrap my arms around her slender body and hold her against me.

"I'm just worried, Max. Gem has felt so bad lately and went to the doctor today. It's bound to be bad news if they want us all together."

"Let's not jump to conclusions. It's no telling with those two." Even though I'm worried, I don't want Tiba to know. That would only make her more concerned than she already is. "How about we jump in the shower and then we'll head on out to the farm."

"Shower together?" Tiba backs up from me and cocks one eyebrow. With one hand on her hip, she gives me her trademark smirk. "And how is that going to work to speed things up?"

I tilt back my head and laugh. This woman already has me figured out. And I love it. And I love her. I love her so damn much that I don't even know how to make her understand. I grab her waist and pull her back to me, kissing her hard.

"I promise no funny business." I stand up from the bed, grab my cane, and pull her behind me toward the bathroom. Glancing over my shoulder, I add, "Only because I'm still injured."

Tiba giggles behind me. It's such a wonderful sound. I know she's worried about Gemma but at least I can take her mind off of it for a minute. I turn on the water in my shower, so it can warm and grab us a couple of towels out of the cabinet.

"This bathroom is amazing! When we have more time, I want to take a long bath in that big old tub. And your shower is crazy! How many shower heads are in there?" Tiba has her head inside the shower. It's big enough that it doesn't need a door. It's just one big tiled corner of the room.

"Ten body jets. And when we have time, I'll introduce you to just how fun those can be." I flash a smile at her.

She spins around toward me. "I'll take you up on that, big guy."

I love that she is already comfortable enough with me, and with us, that she talks about things we will do together. I was so worried she would reject me, but here we are. I plant a quick kiss on the top of her head and after ensuring that the water temperature is perfect, pull her in the shower with me.

As hard as it is, I keep my promise and hand Tiba the soap. "If we touch each other in here, we aren't going to be headed to the farm anytime soon."

She gives me a broad smile as she nods in agreement. We hurriedly get through with the shower and are soon dressed and ready to go. Her smiles are gone and replaced with a frown. I know she is worried, so the sooner I get her to the farm the better. I make quick work of locking the house and slowly work my way to her car. She moves quickly and has the door open for me before I get close.

"You know you're messing with my manhood.

I'm supposed to do that for you."

"Next time, big guy. Just in a hurry this time. Plus, I worked you over in there and felt like you might need a little help." I get a tiny smirk and a wink from her.

"Yes, you did. And I enjoyed every minute of it." I lean down and kiss her. Just a soft quick kiss and it seems to calm her. Once I'm settled in her car, she jumps in her side and we head down the drive-way.

Tiba is quiet as she drives. I notice her down-turned lips and frown have returned, so I make small talk with her. We joke about her having to use my soap that she calls "man smell." I promise to get some girlie stuff for her to keep at my house. The casual banter back and forth about mundane things seems to do the trick with her as she smiles and jokes with me. Again, I am hit with that feeling of amazement that we are so comfortable together to be discussing bath soap for my house.

Before I know it, Tiba turns into the drive for my parents' house. It is a long driveway, more like a road, to get to their house. Since it's gravel, she has to slow down and as we do, her anxiety ramps up again. She has both hands on the wheel and her dark skin is almost white at the knuckles as she grips the steering wheel. I reach over and rub the back of her neck to ease some of her stress.

"Hey. It's going to be okay. I don't like seeing you so worked up."

"You don't understand, Max. Gemma is all I've had for so long. I can't lose her to some illness."

"You aren't going to lose her. This could be nothing. And I'm here for you. So, whatever happens, you won't be alone. I'll be with you." I lean across the console of her small car and kiss her cheek.

When we make it to the house, my parents are both on the porch in the huge rocking chairs my mother loves so much. Tiba parks the car and is around to my side before I can get out. Once I'm out and standing, I grab her hand with my free one. She looks at our hands and then to me before looking to the porch. I can read the question in her eyes.

"I love you, Tiba. They know it. I want them to know we are together. Hell, I want everyone to know." I lift her hand to my lips and kiss it. "Let's go see my folks."

A bright smile crosses her lips as we walk toward the house. She loves my parents and they love her. I'm glad to see the smile on her face. I'm even more glad to see the smile on my mom's face when she sees us together. Mom jumps from her rocker and runs toward us, grabbing Tiba in a hug.

"Does this mean what I think it means?" Mom looks from me to Tiba and back.

"Yes, Mom." I smile at Tiba before looking back to my mother. "Tiba and I have worked things out and are together. And as far as I'm concerned, we are together for good."

"I'm so happy!" my mother squeals. Yes, she actually squeals. She grabs Tiba again and I'm forced to let go of her hand, so she can return the hug.

"Congratulations, son." Dad shakes my hand and then hugs me. "I'm glad Tiba was able to get over your ridiculous behavior and give you a second chance."

Everyone laughs at Dad, even me. He's right and

I can't deny it. I'm so happy she is willing to give me another chance.

"Me too, Dad. And this time, I won't screw it up." I glance at Tiba. "Well, I'll do my best not to, but if I do, call me out on it and don't let me get away with it."

"Seems I did call you out on it," Dad says dryly.

That's my dad. He's always going to tell you like it is. Tiba slips her hand back in mine as we again laugh at my father's joke. Even if it isn't a joke. Sometimes you just have to laugh at the truth because it hurts too much if you don't. Dad is the main reason that I came to my senses.

We all chatter as we walk into the house. Mom leads everyone into the kitchen where she has snacks on the table. Only my mother would make snacks for something like this.

"Snacks, Mom?" I give her a smirk.

She swats me on the shoulder. "Yes, son. Snacks. Food makes everything better." Her smile falters. "I just don't know what they could need to tell us that has to be done together."

Tiba wrinkles her forehead and her grip on my hand tightens. She looks up at me and I see concern written in her brown eyes. I miss the gold flecks in them. It seems they fade away when she is sad or concerned. I'm about to say something when the front door of the house flies open. All eyes turn that direction as Charley runs into the room. She spots us in the kitchen and barrels our direction.

"I'm havin' a baby! I'm havin' a baby!" Charley yells as she runs to Dad and jumps into his arms.

We all look at each other, questions on our faces.

The screen door opens again and Raef and Gemma come inside. They are both smiling which takes the worry out of my mind.

"Well, it sounds like our little one has given away our news." Raef puts his arm around Gemma and pulls her to him before he looks at Charley. "Except, Charlotte isn't having a baby, she's getting a baby."

Confused, I look at Tiba, then Gemma, then my mother. Mom has her hands over her mouth as tears stream down her face. She grabs Gemma and Raef and pulls them to her. I look back at Tiba and she is all smiles. It finally hits me...Gemma is pregnant.

"I'm so happy for you two, well three!" Mom gushes. "When did you find out?"

"I've been sick for so long and Raef has tried to get me to go to the doctor. I finally went today and I'm not sick, I'm just pregnant." Gemma blushes.

"We didn't even think about that possibility. We were as shocked as you are." Raef glances around at everyone.

"Well, all kinds of congratulations in order today." Dad shakes Raef's hand and hugs Gemma, all with Charley still in his arms. He tilts his head in the direction of me and Tiba. "Those two just showed up and told us they are back together and now your news. Good day all around."

Tiba lets go of my hand and hugs Gemma. They hold each other and laugh and cry. I watch in amazement. What is it about women? Why do they always cry when they're happy? I shake my head and chuckle. Turning away from them, I shake Raef's hand.

"Congrats, man. I'm happy for you." I look at Charley who is in my father's ear chattering away with some story. "How's that little one with it?"

"Well, as you heard, she thinks she's having a baby." Raef laughs. "Seriously, though. We were worried. But she took it like a champ and is excited. She just can't decide if she wants a brother or sister."

"I want a brother AND a sister!" Charley calls from across the room. That child has amazing hearing. And she can hear multiple conversations at once. We all laugh, all except Raef and Gemma. They both look like they could be sick.

"No, Charlotte. Just one baby." Raef holds his stomach and looks at Gemma. I laugh harder as I watch him.

"Just one." Gemma looks from Raef to Charley. "Just one."

Our laughter finally catches on with the two of them. Charley frowns in frustration while she tries to figure out what all the adults find so funny. I reach over and take her from my dad. Her bottom lip sticks out as she pouts.

"But I want both," Charley whines in my arms. I squeeze her and kiss her little cheek.

"Well, munchkin, I think your mom & dad just want one baby and most of the time that's all you get."

"But I want both, Uncle Max!"

"I know, sweetie. You'll just have to get one this time and get your mom and dad to have you another one later." I grin at Raef and Gemma.

"Max! Don't tell her that!" Gemma exclaims. "Let's get through this one first!"

"Let's do that, Daddy! Let's have another one

right after this one." Charley reaches for her father and jumps into his arms from mine. The room erupts into laughter again.

"Well, maybe. We'll see after this one." Raef cuts a sideways glance at Gemma who glares at him. "One at a time, little mama. One at a time."

Tiba wanders back beside me and I slide my arm around her waist to pull her closer to me. I can't help but wonder how she really feels about all of this now that I know she can't have children. I lean down to whisper in her ear while everyone is occupied with Charley.

"You okay?" I kiss her ear just because I can.

"I really am." She smiles and turns her head toward me and I capture her lips. Right at the moment I kiss her, my mom notices and clears her throat. Tiba giggles and I chuckle and pull back from her.

"Sorry, Mom."

"Well, now that we know Gemma and Raef's news and I know you two are back together, I'm thinking there may be a chance for a grandchild from my son after all."

Mom smiles, but my face falls. I feel Tiba stiffen next to me. My grip on her tightens and I see her head drop as she looks at the floor. I don't know what to do or say, so I don't do anything but hold on to Tiba. Mom notices that the mood has changed and looks from me to Tiba and back.

"Um, did I say something wrong? I know you just got back together, but I thought you . . . I'm sorry, I'll just stop talking now." Mom's smile is gone and the others in the room are all focused on us. This is not where I wanted this conversation to go.

Tiba takes a deep breath and lifts her head. She turns to me and smiles before she turns back to the group.

"I have something that you all need to know," Tiba begins. I stop her and turn her body to face me.

"You don't have to do this now."

"I know, Max. But I've kept too much secret for too long. If we are going to be together, your parents deserve to know." My sweet girl stands on her tip-toes and kisses me. She gives me one of her radiant smiles and turns away from me, back to face the others. "I've never told anyone until today when I told Max, but I can't have children."

There are gasps around the room. My mom covers her mouth and turns blood red, obviously embarrassed about her previous statement. Gemma runs directly to Tiba and embraces her tightly. I keep one hand on Tiba's back, just to let her know that I'm there for her. My girl is the strongest person I know.

"Oh, Tiba! Why didn't you tell me before?" Gemma cries as she holds on to her.

"I never felt the need to talk about it. I honestly never thought there would be a man in my life for it to matter." Tiba slides out of Gemma's arms and turns back into mine, looking up at me with the gold flecks shining in her eyes. "Now, with Max, it became important for everyone to know."

"I'm so sorry. I wouldn't have said what I said if I knew. I'm so sorry." Mom sobs as she speaks. I'm not really sure if it is all because of what she said or if part of it is because she knows I won't be giving her any grandchildren. At least, not in the traditional way.

Gazing down into Tiba's eyes, I let her know how proud of her I am. I take both of her hands in mine, bring them to my lips, and kiss both of them before I look back to my parents. Mom's cries while Dad stands stoically to the side.

"Look, Mom and Dad. I know this is a shock to you, but Tiba and I discussed this and it's not an issue with me. I love her and that's it. She's all I need. If, and I mean if, we decide down the road that we want children, then we'll adopt. Simple as that. For now, all we need is each other and time together."

Dad walks up to me and grips my shoulder. He watches us for a moment, then smiles.

"I'm proud of you, son." He nods at me and then looks at Tiba. "I'm sorry you've been through so much. Don't ever let this define you. If you two want kids, there's lots of them out there that need good parents."

The mood in the room that was jubilant a few moments ago is now somber. Everyone is quiet, and no one knows what to say. Tiba and I are the only ones still smiling. We gaze at each other, our hands still clasped together, like two people who can't get enough of each other. But then again, that's what we are.

"Why'd everyone stop talking?" And just like that, the silence is broken by none other than Charley.

"Charley!" Gemma cries. Tiba and I laugh, and I wave my hand in Gemma's direction to stop her from chastising Charley.

"Auntie T had something she needed to tell everyone, and it made them sad for a minute, but now they know they don't have to be sad." Charley watches me as I talk to her, her little nose scrunched up while she tries to understand.

"So, Auntie T isn't sad?"

"No, munchkin, Auntie T isn't sad, and neither is Uncle Max." I smile at the precocious four-year old. "In fact, we are very, very happy. And we are very happy you are getting a little sister or brother."

"I'm glad you're not sad Auntie T." Charley smiles at Tiba while she sits in Raef's arms. She looks at Gemma and huffs, that bottom lip slips back out. "But I still want a sister AND a brother."

We all laugh as Charley drops her head down on Raef's shoulder. Even Gemma and Raef laugh this time. Mom slips over to me and hugs me before doing the same to Tiba.

"As long as you are happy, I'm happy." Mom holds her palm to my cheek. She pats my cheek a couple of times and turns back toward Gemma. "And besides, if Charley has her way, we are going to get plenty of grandchildren from those two over there." She tilts her head toward Raef and Gemma.

"Sounds like it." Tiba laughs and I join in with her. She leans her body against mine and I wrap my arm around her middle, holding her against me. She tilts her head back against my chest and looks up to see my face.

"I think everyone is ganging up on us Raef." Gemma finally giggles.

"Yep, Gem. I think so."

"More babies, Mommy!" Charley says as she drifts off to sleep in Raef's arms.

My gaze is still on Tiba and hers on me. The rest of the room fades away. I hear the laughter and the chatter, but none of it registers. It's only Tiba there with me. She's everything I didn't know I wanted, but once I found her, I can't live without her. I drop a kiss on her upturned forehead.

"How about you and I get out of here and take this party back to my house? We have a lot of catching up to do." I waggle my eyebrows.

Tiba laughs and stands up straighter. "That we do, big guy. That we do." She grabs my hand and I readily take hers.

We quickly say our goodbyes to my parents and Raef and Gemma. We each gently kiss Charley on the cheek since she is still asleep. Both of us share our excitement of the new expected little one with Raef and Gemma one more time before we leave. Everyone follows us outside, even though we want to make a quick getaway. After we finally make our way to Tiba's car, we are able to slip inside it and watch everyone go back inside the house.

"Whew. Wasn't sure we were going to get out of there." I have my head rested on the back of the seat turned toward Tiba in the driver's seat.

"I know! But I love them all. They are our family and I love that we are that important to them." She smiles as she starts the car. I reach out and stop her before she puts it in gear. She turns to me, questions on her face.

"I just wanted one more kiss before we go." She leans into me and I kiss her with everything I have. "You, Tiba Ramon, you are my family. Along with those crazies we just left. I love you."

"I love you too, Max." She smiles and kisses me

again. "Now, let's get home and start catching up."

Home. As Tiba takes us back toward the highway, I think of that one word. Home. She just used that word to describe my house, our home. She may not live there with me yet, but I am so happy to hear she already thinks of it as home.

This woman that I kissed in a barn has turned my life upside down. She has shown me what true love is. I drop my hand over the console to rest on her leg as she drives. She smiles without looking at me when she feels my touch. We ride silently, my gaze never leaving her, as we drive home. Home to not only catch up but to begin our future. Home with each other.

Epilogue

TIBA

TEN BOXES SIT IN THE living room of Max's house. Well, *our* house now. Max was finally able to lose the cane yesterday and he insisted that we not wait any longer to move the rest of my things to the house. I'm still amazed that this beautiful place is my home now.

"That's the last one." Max closes the door behind him. "Are you sure this is all you want from your old place? We have plenty of room here."

"I'm sure. The women's shelter is going to pick up the furniture and the rest of the stuff that's left. We don't need it here and they can definitely use it." When Max first asked me to move in with him, I knew what I wanted to do with my things. The only things I wanted to bring with me had some type of meaning. "I want a fresh start here, for us."

Max slides his arm around my waist and pulls me flush against his body. My hands slide under his t-shirt and find the glorious muscles of his chest.

"Have I mentioned lately how glad I am that you are here with me?" Max asks as he kisses my neck over and over.

"Hmmm. Not today."

His lips work his way up to nip my ear. "Well, I am so very happy." Max whispers in my ear. "This house is *our* home now."

"Ours," I repeat.

Max continually reminds me that his house is now ours because I keep referring to it as *his* house. As at home as I feel here, I still have to remind myself that this *is* my home and not just his. Sometimes I can't wrap my head around the fact that I live with Max Greenwood. My prince charming swept me off my feet and into his home.

"If you keep kissing me like that, these boxes are going to stay in the middle of the floor." I pull back from Max and look at the mess in the room.

"I wouldn't mind that. You know I can be distracted with you anytime." He chuckles.

"One track mind, big guy. Let's get this finished and then we'll talk about doing the fun stuff." Pointing to a stack of boxes for him, I grab one closest to me. "Grab a couple and let's get these unpacked."

Max and I spend the next several hours unpacking my things and meshing them in the house with his. Although I try to convince him to leave his wall décor in the living room, he won't have it. He removes everything from the walls and replaces them with the photos I have taken and framed over the years. I had way more than I could hang on the walls of my little apartment and he is so excited to put them all here in our house.

"There." Max hangs the last photo in the living room. "Now, it's home for both of us."

"They look great in here, Max. You didn't have to do this, though. Your walls were amazing as they were."

"I know. But I wanted to. I've loved your work since the first time I walked into your apartment. This is our home, baby. I love how they look here." He lays the hammer on the small table against the wall.

"Thank you." I blush as Max pushes my hair behind my ear. "Thank you for sharing your home with me."

"Our home, baby. Ours. Yours and mine." He kisses me softly. My eyes drift closed and reach for him, but my hands don't connect with anything. My eyes pop open to find him in front of me on one knee, a tiny box in his hand. "This isn't when or how I planned to do this, but I just can't wait."

My hands fly to my face, covering my mouth in shock. Tears form in my eyes as Max eases the cover of the box open and I see the most beautiful diamond ring. My gaze raises from the box to find him staring at me. His green eyes shine as brightly as the diamond.

"Tiba, I'm not a man with lots of romantic words. But, I know I love you. And I want to spend every day of the rest of my life with you. Will you make it official and marry me?"

"Yes!" My hands drop from my face as I say the one word that he waits to hear. A smile spreads across his face. "Yes, Max, yes! I will marry you!"

He takes the ring from the box and places the closed box on the table by the hammer. He eases up from his knee to stand in front of me. As he reaches for my left hand, I raise it toward him. He holds it gently in one hand while he slides the ring on with the other. My eyes are glued to my finger the entire time. Once he has the ring in place, he raises my hand to his lips and kisses my finger right below the ring.

"I love you, Tiba." He has unshed tears in his eyes as he gazes down at me.

"I love you, too, Max." My arms snake around his body and hug him with all my strength. His arms slip around me and we stand that way for several minutes, just holding each other.

Finally, I pull away from him and hold my hand up to admire the ring that now adorns my finger. It's an amazing emerald cut diamond with smaller diamonds around the entire band. It's the most beautiful ring I've ever seen.

"Do you like it?" Max asks.

"Like it? I love it! It's so beautiful!" I smile at him, dropping my hand back to hold his.

"When I saw it, I knew it was the one for you. It's shiny and sparkly, everything you are."

"Thank you, Max. For the ring, for asking me to marry you, but most of all, for loving me." Stretching on my tip-toes, I reach up to kiss him. He wraps his arms tightly around me and lifts me against him to where our faces are level with each other. After a passionate kiss, he pulls his face back just enough to look me in the eyes. His lips are still so close to mine, I can feel his words when he talks.

"No, Tiba, thank you. I never could've imagined a life like we have." Max kisses me again before he eases his lips away from mine and gives me a wicked grin. "How about we go celebrate now?"

"That sounds like a plan, big guy." I laugh as Max turns my body in his arms and carries me toward the bedroom. Our bedroom, in our home.

Acknowledgements

As always, I want to thank my husband for sup-porting me in my dream of writing. His constant support and patience with my writing keeps me on track.

I also want to thank my children for their support. Although none of them want to actually read the books I write, they support me by shar-ing them with others. Our children are all adults and say that they don't want to know where their mom/step-mom comes up with certain *aspects* of the stories.

This book has a good bit of medical issues that occur, and I couldn't have written them without the help of my favorite nurse, Brandy Montpelier. Thank you for all of your help!

A big thanks goes out to Renita and Curtis at A Book a Day for their invaluable help with the development of this book. The two of you made this story even better.

A special thanks to The Killion Group, Inc. for their work on the cover, blurb, editing and format-ting. These ladies do a phenomenal job and I don't know what I would do without them.

Last but certainly not least, thanks to you, my readers. Thank you for supporting my dream by purchasing my books. You make it possible to tell my stories. Without readers, stories are written in silence.

About the Author

Growing up in rural Louisiana, I dreamed of one day being a writer. Although it took many years to achieve that dream, life has been fulfilling along the way. Being a wife and a mother are the things I consider my biggest accomplishments. My family is number one in my eyes.

I am retired from working in public school finance. In addition to writing, I enjoy reading, photography, and traveling. I am obsessed with all things Disney and Thirty Seconds to Mars. In addition to my husband and son, my three favorite men are Shannon Leto, Jared Leto and Mickey Mouse.

CONNECT WITH C. KAYE

Email:
authorckaye@gmail.com

Website:
www.authorckaye.wixsite.com/ckaye

Facebook:
www.facebook.com/authorckaye

Twitter:
www.twitter.com/authorckaye

Instagram:
www.instagram.com/authorc.kaye/

Other Books by C. Kaye:

THIS TIME AROUND
(Our Time for Love #1)

WEDDING TIME: A NOVELLA
(Our Time for Love #1.5)